Goodbye, Bobby Thomson! Goodbye, John Wayne!

ALAN S. FOSTER

SIMON AND SCHUSTER · NEW YORK

Published by Simon and Schuster
Rockefeller Center, 630 Fifth Avenue
New York, New York 10020

First printing

SBN 671-21357-1
Library of Congress Catalog Card Number: 72-90390
Manufactured in the United States of America
by H. Wolff Book Mfg. Co., Inc.

For Sue

CONTENTS

PART ONE

The Kid

(1951)

1

My old man was a baseball fan first, a Giant fan second. He liked nothing better than traveling into the city, going all the way up to the Polo Grounds, then sitting in the same section of the upper deck (halfway between home plate and first) and scoring each game methodically. He never said too much during a game, he just held his scorecard and stared quietly down at the action below. Some people get all excited at baseball games. Some go just about out of their mind. Not my old man, though. He just liked to sit there and score. Once in a very rare while he'd jump to his feet and stick his fist up into the air, and quite often he would applaud a good play—whether the Giants made it or not—but usually he never said a word during a game except to ask me if I had to go to the bathroom. A lot of Giant fans were like that in those days: baseball fans first, Giant fans second.

That's probably why I preferred football.

And Chuck? Old Chuck didn't know the first thing about baseball. Or football. Or any kind of organized sport. He just didn't go for that professional crap. And Chuck was right, even though it took me over ten years to find it out. Even if he did die before I knew what was what. Someplace in Korea it was. I don't know where exactly. It doesn't make much difference now, but it sure made a lot of difference then, because that's why we were there, really—that's why Dad and I were up at the Polo Grounds: because of Chuck.

The government claimed they had found the remains of Chuck's body and, as a convenience to us, they shipped these remains—now ashes—back to New Jersey so that we could bury him on Monday up at a cemetery in Montclair. It was bad enough getting the word several weeks before about his being missing in action, but it was worse when the official telegram came telling my folks that it was all over, that there was no use in hoping for the best, that Chuck wasn't missing any longer—he was just dead. They could have left things at that, but no, an election year was coming up so they had to follow everything until it came down to its logical conclusion, right? They had to screw everything up and send us this olive drab-colored box full of ashes. Chuck's ashes. Who knows whose ashes they really were? Who cared? Chuck was dead, that's all that mattered.

I didn't know anyone else who died in Korea, but I do know that Chuck had no business being there, no business being in the Army, no business dying. Hell, he didn't even believe in the war. He was Republican through and through and said that the whole thing had been completely illegal. But look where he was and look what happened to him. Illegal!

I remember the day he went off and joined the Army, all right. We'd all been down at the shore, down at these cottages just north of Seaside Heights. I had just finished my junior year of high school and we had been out on the beach—tossing a football around because it was too cold to swim—when Kitsie Watts came running out of the girls' house saying that it was war. "War," she shouted to us. "WAR!"

We couldn't have cared less at the time, mainly, I think, because we all had another year of school left, at the very least, but we did ask where this particular war was.

"Korea," she shouted. We went back to playing around with the football because Kitsie was always getting excited about things like that. She was about the only Democrat in the whole high school, except for Mary Lou Lawson, and Mary Lou was colored. Come to think of it, the only colored people we had in our high school either played football or were Democrats, or both. Kitsie was a nice girl, though, and got along with everyone, mainly because she had these big knockers. She and BB Johnson had the biggest knockers in our class, and always had had ever since the sixth grade.

Anyway, Kitsie came out there and told us that somebody had pushed down into Korea and that we were all going to war. Not that it made any real difference to us—what the hell, we knew war was just something you saw in the movies, or read about in the comic books, or something real good like that. I mean to us, right there on that Jersey beach in June, 1950, war was just something we always won, just like football games. I'd had a cousin in World War II, but he never talked about it, so all I knew about World War II was that we whipped the Germans and Japs, that my parents hadn't cared all that much about rationing, and that Chuck had had a lot of fun on Boy Scout paper drives. It might have affected us more if the Germans or Japs had actually bombed Northwood, New Jersey, but then the Germans and Japs weren't all that dumb. All Northwood, New Jersey, cared about was high school football on Saturdays, church on Sundays, and catching the 7:37 on weekdays. It was a funny town all right. I remember going to a football rally before the Plainfield game in 1944, and before the ceremonies got under way, they showed a newsreel and in the newsreel there were some shots of Hitler giving a speech or something. No one in the theater said a word. Then, a little later, FDR came on the screen. You should have heard all the noise! If there was anything except booing I sure didn't hear it. It was really something, but that was my old hometown.

I never used to get excited one way or the other politically. I suppose I would have voted Republican because everyone else in my family did, but I never really understood what was going on. I don't think my family did, either. Most of the time I didn't even talk about politics, or current events, or things like that. I didn't even like to talk about the war. What I did talk about was sports. Yes, I can honestly say that I did talk about sports.

The day Kitsie came out and told us about Korea was the last day of our stay at the shore, and driving back up to Northwood we listened to the news on the radio. It still didn't affect us one way or the other, except that we knew the Communists were bad, and that we were good.

When I got back to my house on Effingham Place, I barged right in shouting that we were At War and had everyone heard the exciting news? It seemed that everyone had heard the exciting news. In fact, my mother and my father were really upset about everything.

Chuck was home from Cornell and he said, yes, he knew all about Korea and that he was going to sign up. I guess this really shocked me 'cause Chuck was the last person in the world I thought would sign up. My mother and father were pretty upset about it, too, but somehow I think that they thought Chuck would be turned down, or change his mind, or something like that. But Chuck didn't change his mind and he did sign up. He was sent down to Fort Dix and then about four months later he was shipped overseas with the 9th Infantry Division.

One weekend in October, before he was moved out, he got a pass and saw me score two TDs against Roselle Park. The next day we drove him back to Dix. My mother kept saying that he wouldn't be sent to Korea because of his size, but Chuck had told me the night before—after I'd come home from the Victory Dance at the Y—that he was definitely going to Frozen Chosen. He said he still didn't think the war was legal, but that he wanted to get over there and get the stupid thing over with. We talked quite a bit that night. He admitted that he had had a rough time in basic training, and I guess he must have been picked on a whole lot. Chuck was always being picked on. In Northwood if you didn't play some sport, or were valedictorian of your class, why you weren't thought too highly of. It was stupid, but that's how it was. All Chuck really cared about was botany and geology and things like that. He was Republican through and through, but he wasn't a real bug on the subject. My old man was a real bug on the subject, but all Chuck cared about was if things were legal or not.

I got a couple of letters from him my senior year and then one right before I left for Columbus. He told me that it was pretty cold over in Korea, but he didn't say anything at all about what he was actually doing. I don't even know how he died, really, or what happened to him. My old man called me up at the dorm after practice one night when he got word about Chuck being missing in action. He said he hadn't told Mom, 'cause there was still a chance everything would be OK. It didn't really hit me that Chuck might actually never come back home. I knew that a lot of guys were dying in Korea, but I never thought that Chuck would be one of them. He was always such a quiet, studious sort of guy—not like the guys who get killed in the movies at all. Come to think of it, though, maybe he *was* like the guys who get killed in the movies. It's those John Wayne types who never get killed.

It didn't bother me so much at first, knowing that Chuck was missing in action. I was shook up, but I wasn't all that shook up. I mean I was having problems myself at the time—somehow I just hadn't fit in at State. And I was having trouble with the football, too. It seemed like the whole state of Ohio was trying out for the team that year and I wasn't getting much of a chance to do anything. One day they even got the idea that they were going to convert me to guard. They said I was fast enough for running guard, but not fast enough for fullback. Maybe it was partly because they had ten or eleven other fullbacks, all bigger and faster than I was. Maybe because I'd never played the T-formation before—all we had used in high school was the single wing. I don't know. I do know that I was plenty unhappy being passed over, not getting a real chance to show what I could do. They didn't cut me from the team, but they didn't seem overjoyed to have me around, either. Some of the trouble was due to the fact that I had been recruited by a coaching staff entirely different from the staff they then had. So, when I got the final word about Chuck it was an opportunity for me to bug out, to get away from Ohio, to get back to New Jersey—even if it was only for my brother's funeral.

I went in to talk to the coach before I left. At first, I was just going to write a note to the freshman coordinator, but then I saw Smokey in his office so I went right in and told him that my brother had been killed in Korea. Right away he got all upset and said, sure I should go home, that I shouldn't even think of anything else. He called the airport up for me and I think he even ended up paying for my ticket. It was really sort of embarrassing in a way; Chuck had actually died maybe three or four weeks earlier, and I was bugging out not out of sadness for my brother, but because I was fed up with Ohio in general, and OSU football in particular.

But I have to say this, Smokey was great about the whole thing. He really was. I'd never really liked him before that. He used to stare at me in practice, and shout, and say I didn't have the right attitude or anything. He was right, though, I didn't have the right attitude. I guess I was too used to being the high school big shot, the hero of all Northwood, New Jersey. All my life I'd grown up looking forward to playing on the Northwood varsity, and then when I did play on the varsity for two and a half years, it was pretty good—not what I imagined it to be, but pretty good. But high school football was one thing, college something else. I really think I should have been forced to do other things in Northwood besides play football, but that's all I really ever did. Or thought about.

So, everything considered, it was sort of a relief for me when Chuck died: I could get away from Ohio and go back home. Even if there wasn't a formal funeral, there was this ceremony down at Dix and then they were going to bury Chuck's ashes up in Montclair. So it was reason enough to go home, right?

Sure it was reason enough to go home.

My folks didn't really expect me (my Dad had said on the phone that it would be all right if I stayed in Columbus), but I barged right in on them that Saturday afternoon. Northwood was playing Bound Brook that day and I had sort of hoped to make it in time for the game, but it took me longer to get from Idlewild to Northwood than it did to get all the way from Columbus to New York.

When I walked in the door I expected to see my old man listening to the Cornell game on the radio, and smell my mother cooking something. But they were just sitting there when I arrived, just sitting there in the dark living room, not doing anything. My mother rushed over to me when I came in and hugged me like crazy. Dad shook my hand solemnly.

"I'm glad you came," he said.

"You didn't have to come all this way," my mother added, wiping her hand across her face.

I assured them that I had wanted to come.

Over dinner Dad told me how he had gotten the news, how some officer had called, and then a lady from the Red Cross, and then finally the telegram from the President. They both hated Truman like anything, and "his" war, but they were both more sorry than bitter.

I was glad when dinner was over, and a little sorry I had come all the way home.

Later on that evening I went into Chuck's room and looked once more through all his stuff. His room was just the way it always was—full of rocks, and plants, and parts of chemistry sets, and things like that. I looked into his desk, but it was just as messy and crammed full of junk as always. Then I went back into my room and lay down on my own bed and looked up at the ceiling, just thinking about things. After a while, I leaned over and turned on my radio and listened to the football scores. State had beaten SMU and Fred Benners, 7–0. Big deal. The pennant race was going down to the last day in the National League. Who cared about baseball? There weren't any high school scores so I switched the radio off. It felt sort of strange being in my old room again. I got up after a few minutes and went over to my desk, sat down, and then started to look through all of the old letters I kept there. I never threw out old letters. After a while, I found the one I wanted. It was the last letter I ever received from Chuck. It came just before I left for Columbus and preschool practice.

"Hi Bud," he began in his scribbled writing:

Sorry I haven't whipped off a letter to you sooner but I guess you know how things are over here. Things aren't too good over here. First it was cold, now it's hot. You get used to it, my sergeant says.

Enough of the weather report. Are you all set about going out to the Midwest? Try to study hard and don't take football too seriously, at least not your freshman year, anyway. I understand they take it even more seriously out there than they do in downtown Northwood.

Ran into Charlie May a week or so ago. He says to say hello and wants to know if your fumbleitis (?) is cured yet—whatever that is. He's in the Marines and has gone completely bald.

About all for now. They want me going out on patrol again so I guess I better go. They made me a corporal the other day, but it doesn't mean anything. They had to give it to someone and I'm the only one left from my original unit.

I don't know what they're saying about Frozen Chosen in

Northwood, but I know one thing—it really is *important someone is over here.*

Enough of the sermon—write me if you get a chance. Give Mom and Dad my love . . . And best of luck in Columbus.

Your Brother,
Charles

I read the letter twice, then went back to my bed and started to cry. For the first real time it hit me that Chuck was never coming back. I realized then what war was all about, too. Death, that's what war was all about. Chuck had no business being in Korea. He had no business going out on patrol, being made a corporal. He should be alive, that's all. Alive!

Right after I graduated from high school, we all went down to the shore (where else?) and really had a pretty wild time. I remember one night trying, unsuccessfully, to snuggle up close to Kitsie Watts. But Kitsie was more interested in singing some of Those Good Old Songs, so me and some of the other unsuccessful guys charged up and down the dunes, playing like we were all John Waynes, shouting out "Korea" at the top of our lungs like it was Gung-ho!, or Geronimo!, or something special like that.

"Korrrrr—eeeeeeee—aaaaaaaa!" we shouted, slipping and sliding down the dunes, laughing like anything.

"Korrrr—eeeeeee—aaaaaaaa!!"

It was a lot of fun.

Sure it was.

And that's why I cried about Chuck.

After a while my old man came up and knocked on my door, then came into the room.

"Mind if I sit down?" he asked. I shook my head, then turned over and looked at the window so he couldn't see my face. He sat on the edge of the bed and didn't say anything for a few moments. "I'm glad you're here," he said finally, quietly, whispering sort of. "Mom's been having a tough time of it."

I didn't say anything. My father waited for a while, then went on. "It's good to have you home, Pete," he said.

I think we were both embarrassed. At least I was embarrassed. My father and I had always gotten along great, even if he had been a big Giant fan. I mean we had our squabbles, sure, but they were nothing serious. He used to argue with Chuck all the time, but the only thing he argued with me about was football. He had wanted me to go up to Ithaca, but I never really cared much for the Ivy League and, besides, I wanted to play big-time football. My first choice was Penn State and I'm not really sure why I decided to go to OSU. That first month in Columbus I sure wished I had gone to Penn State, let me tell you.

"How long will you be home for, Pete?" Dad asked.

"I don't know." I thought for a few minutes. "I think I'm going to give up football, Dad."

"Give up football! Why?"

"I don't know."

"Think about it," he said seriously. "Think about it."

"I have thought about it."

I felt Dad looking at me, nodding his head like he always did. "I know it must be hard at a big school like Ohio State," he said. "But I'm sure if you stick to it . . ." He stopped and looked away.

"They're making me a guard," I said suddenly.

Dad smiled in a sorrowful sort of way. That explained it, as far as he was concerned, I guess. "So, that's it?" he chuckled, patting my leg and looking at the wall. "So, that's it, huh?" That wasn't it, but I didn't say anything else. "Think it over, son," he said slowly. "Think it over."

I'd already thought it over, plenty, but I also knew that

just then wasn't the best time in the world to talk about it, either. Especially since it was my decision, no one else's.

The next day, Sunday, we all went to church together. The minister gave an inspiring sermon and insinuated that if Tom Dewey hadn't been so arrogant during the last presidential campaign certain members of the congregation might not have been wasted defending a foreign country. Several times I've wanted to raise up my hand in church and ask some questions, but I never had the nerve. I wanted to do it right then, too, but didn't. I'm not sure why I didn't. But those ministers really used to bug me sometimes: getting all excited about holding early services on Thanksgiving so that everyone could get to the annual Turkey Day Classic with Plainfield, our traditional rival, on time. One minister, I remember, even used to pray for a swift "and merciful" victory over our hated adversaries. I often used to wonder if Plainfield ministers did the same thing.

As a kid I liked going to church because I used to have some of my best daydreams there. But as I grew older and as I listened more and more to what was going on, I came to the conclusion that it was all a bunch of crap. Chuck used to say the same thing: "It's all a bunch of crap," he'd whisper to me during the sermon. It was, too, and I would have refused to go except for the fact that BB Johnson went regularly and she took my mind off what was being said.

On the way out of church, the minister shook my hand and nodded at me solemnly, as if he knew, deep down inside, what I was going through. Sure he did. After church, we had a big dinner at home and I could tell that my folks were really glad to have me home because it gave them something to do besides just sit around and think about Chuck. After dinner, I took Dad's car and drove around town, looking at all the old places for a while.

I drove over to Memorial Field and drove around it a

couple of times—looking up at the stands, and the locker room, and the scoreboard—but I didn't stop. I went by Crazy Ed Ringen's house, but I didn't stop there, either. Then I drove over to the Gardens and went by Kitsie Watts' house, and BB Johnson's house, and Doug Dickey's house, but they were all away at college so I didn't stop. Besides, I didn't really want to see anyone, anyway. So I drove back through downtown Northwood, then went home. Mom and Dad were taking naps, so I went into my room and read the Sunday papers while listening halfheartedly to the Giant and Dodger games on the radio. The last day of the season and the teams were tied, but I didn't really care all that much one way or the other. Baseball was still baseball. So I turned the games off, and put the paper down, then tried to think about things. But I just couldn't concentrate on any one thing. No matter what I started out thinking about, I always ended up thinking about Chuck.

Why did they have to go and kill Chuck?

Why?

The next day we drove down to Fort Dix, only when we got there they told us there had been a mix-up and that we couldn't claim Chuck's ashes until Tuesday. My aunt and uncle from Teaneck met us there, but the only other person to show up was Mr. Goucher, the junior high school Latin teacher. He was a nice old guy and adviser for the Nature Club, which Chuck had been a member of, and I liked him even though I had had a tough time with Latin, mainly because it was hard to concentrate on declensions and all that stuff when BB Johnson's ever-growing knockers were just a few inches away from me.

Dad told me that I didn't have to stay around until Tuesday, that I should probably be getting back to Columbus, but I think he was just nervous about my wanting to quit football. I said I wanted to stay, though, and a little later he agreed to let me drive them back down to Fort Dix on Tuesday. My mother couldn't have lasted another day of postponement, and I'm not so sure my father could have, either, so it was good that I was there to drive. But the ceremony went off properly, if late, and we were given some medals and then this olive drab-colored box of ashes. They wouldn't just let us take the box away, though; they insisted that a special car drive up to Montclair with us and that an honor guard witness the box being put into the ground. My aunt and uncle were along again, but Mr. Goucher couldn't make it, so there was only a few of us at this cemetery in Montclair. One of the soldiers blew taps for Chuck, but as far as I was concerned that wasn't Chuck in that box, just some ashes.

Driving back to Northwood I told my Dad that I wanted to join the Army, too. It wasn't such a smart thing to say under the circumstances, but I said it anyway. My mother started to cry, but all Dad did was to get mad.

"You can't join without my permission," he growled.

"I'm eighteen," I answered.

"Ridiculous!" Dad replied.

Personally, I think he was frustrated about Chuck, sure, but I also think he was just as shook up over the fact that the Giants had just lost the second playoff game to the Dodgers, 10-zip. They'd won the first one behind Big Jim Hearn, 3 to 1, but this gave him a chance to let off steam.

"Join the Army," he scoffed. "Boy, is that stupid!"

"I'm going," I mumbled.

"Stupid!"

I don't even know if I wanted to go into the Army or not, but I sure as hell didn't want my old man telling me not to go, even under the circumstances. I didn't particularly want to go back to State, but there wasn't any other place I wanted to go. I mean, it would be nice to go over to Korea and avenge Chuck, John-Wayne-style, but I knew you could only do that sort of thing in the movies, not in real life.

Well, we argued about it back and forth for a while—all the way back to Northwood, in fact—but we didn't come to any firm conclusion. I knew I was hurting my mother something terrible, but that's just the way it had to be. Finally, I agreed to stay over one more day and talk it over with Dad. It was his idea that we go up to the Polo Grounds for the final playoff game; it certainly wasn't mine. And, after the game, we'd talk everything over. Sure we would. I don't know why we couldn't have talked it over at home, but we never seemed to be able to talk things over at home, so the Polo Grounds it had to be.

Dad had to go into his office early, so I didn't take the same train as he did. Mom held onto my arm when I left.

"Please promise me you won't join the Army," she said. "Please promise."

"I can't promise, Mom."

"You will talk to Dad, though?"

"I'll talk to Dad."

"You promise?"

I nodded. "I promise," I said.

She hung onto me a long time before I left. She knew I'd make up my own mind—I always had.

I got into the City about eleven and stashed my bag in a locker, then rode the subway up to Times Square. Everywhere I went everyone seemed to be talking about the big game—Giants versus Dodgers, Maglie against Newcombe, the winner ending up National League champion. Big fuckin' deal. I walked over to the Music Hall and found out I didn't have enough time to see the new show there, *An American in Paris* with Gene Kelly. I was sorry about this 'cause Chuck and I had always liked going into the Music Hall and sitting way down front so that we could see all the

Rockettes talking to each other during the stage show. I didn't want to only see half a show, though, so I walked up Fifth Avenue for a while, then cut across the park and picked up the AA train at the 72nd Street station. I liked taking the AA up to 155th Street and then walking down to the Polo Grounds from Coogan's Bluff. Dad always took the D train; most people did.

I met him outside the ball park, then we went in and found our seats. He apologized for only being able to get seats out in the lower left-field stands, but it didn't make all that much difference.

We watched infield practice and ate some hot dogs for lunch and I thought for a while that it might rain, but even though it was dark and cloudy, the rain never came. After a while we stood up for the National Anthem and then, all of a sudden, the game was underway. Old Number 35, Sal the Barber Maglie, took the mound for the Giants. He looked sharp when he warmed up, but he wasn't so sharp a little later. With one out, Reese walked. Then Duke Snider also walked.

"Oh, those bases on balls," Dad mumbled.

Jackie Robinson came to the plate and the crowd started to make a whole lot of noise. The stands were only about three-quarters full and there must have been just as many Dodger fans there as there were Giant rooters. Maybe it just seemed that way 'cause Giant fans never made too much noise. C'mon, I urged Jackie. Hit it the fuck out of here right now!

He connected sharply on the first pitch—not good enough for a homer, but good enough to drive Reese home. One run. One big run. The Dodgers were on their way!

And I made up my mind right then and there. But I didn't say anything. Not yet. Then, in the second inning, the Giants came to bat, still down one-zip. Some of the fans started to clap—even my old man. Lockman started off with a single. Then Bobby Thomson came up and belted a line drive base hit to left. Lockman dashed around second, then held up. My old man was on his feet, his fist up in the air. But then he sank slowly back into his seat. Thomson had raced around first and dug for second—not seeing that Lockman had stopped running. He tried to get back to first, but was tagged out in an easy rundown. My old man didn't say anything, he just wrote it all out methodically in his scorecard. The Giants had had their chance, but had failed.

"Dad," I said softly.

He looked over at me, shaking his head sadly.

"I definitely want to join the Army," I stated.

"Not now," he said impatiently, a little surprised at my statement. "Later."

"No," I said, getting angry. "Now!" He started to shake his head again, but I wouldn't let him say anything. "I'm going into the Army and that's all there is to it!"

2

It might not have been the best place in the world to have a good father-son discussion, but it wasn't the worst, either. There we were, sitting in the goddam Polo Grounds having our first real heart-to-heart talk. It seems kind of funny now, but it wasn't so funny then. All we'd ever talked about before was football. Chuck and Dad were always arguing about politics, but whenever I tried to say something, they'd just sort of look at me for a moment or two and not say anything in return.

In fact, my old man never even told me about the birds and bees, as they say. Once or twice I think he had the idea on his mind, but he never actually got around to it. The closest he ever came was one summer after I graduated from junior high school when he slipped this book into my bureau drawer, underneath my underwear. It sort of bugged me that he didn't come out and say, here, read this, or tell me what was what—no, he had to slip it under my old underwear and jocks. In a way, though, I was glad we never did have that big talk—I know it would have embarrassed hell out of both of us.

I'm not even so sure that it's a good idea having your own father telling you about it anyway. I think an impartial observer might be best—or anyone not an immediate member of the family.

By the time my old man got around to sneaking in this textbook on the subject, though, I was well on my way over the hill. Maybe not completely, but at least I'd been all the way to the threshold by that time and had had one good opportunity. That was when I had been fourteen years old, too.

I was going with BB Johnson at the time and we were both going to this same dancing class on Wednesday afternoons at the Tennis Club. We used to dance real close during all the blackout dances and then, one New Year's Eve in Dick Brady's basement, we danced some more. This time we couldn't have danced any closer, mainly because we knew that Mrs. Mulford, the dancing lady, wouldn't be able to come around and shine a flashlight at us as she liked to do at the Club. So dance securely we did, and I managed to get my hand in between us, holding BB's hand in real close, see, so that the back of my hand was up against one of her knockers. Oh, she really liked that; and so did I. She kept trying to press me closer and closer—and, my, everything was so very nice.

And then this jerk, Alan goddam Lampton, turned the lousy lights on and everyone laughed at us two, red-faced lovers, and we had nothing else to do but to just laugh right back at them. A little later on in the evening I tried to catch someone else copping a feel, but everyone was on his guard by then. The next Sunday, BB sat next to me in church and during the Morning Prayer asked me over to her house for dinner. Naturally, off to her house I went. After dinner, BB's parents had to go out someplace so we had to wash the dishes. When we were done, BB said that I had better go, but she didn't make me go, so I stuck around and read the papers with her. Then, after a little hemming and hawing, I asked her if maybe she wanted to dance or something. She smiled at me and said, sure, why not? So we went down into her cellar, which was a game room, and put on some records and started to dance. It was very nice, but somehow it just wasn't the same. It's different when it's dark, 'cause when it's daytime you can still see each other and, I don't know, it's just better in the dark, that's all. After a while, though, we worked our hands up in between our hot little bodies and I'd apply a little pressure with my finger ever so often, and BB would do the same in response, and then I opened my eyes and looked at her, only she didn't see me 'cause her eyes were still closed.

Well, this was all very nice, but after a while I got to thinking that maybe we had better stop right there, or else go the full route—whatever exactly the full route was. So, we stopped dancing, and sat down on the leather couch, and when I put my arm around her she sort of cuddled up real close to me and then the next thing I knew we were kissing away real good. After a few false starts, I sort of laid my hand on top of one of BB's knockers, ready to whip it off at the very first sign of resistance. There wasn't any sign of resistance at all, though; in fact, BB took her hand and put it very gently on top of mine, sighing at the very same time I sighed. Great! Tremendous! But where do you go from there, Dad?

It's probably a good thing that my old man had never gone through the whole procedure with me 'cause I sure as hell would have gone through it with BB that time. Fortunately, her sister came in so we didn't have any opportunity—then. A few weeks later, though, we made a date at church to do our homework together at her house. Her parents were home this time, but it didn't seem to bother BB at all. We went down into the cellar and opened up our books and turned on the record player and pretty soon, and I'm not exactly sure just how, I was laying on top of her. I jumped off a few seconds later when BB's mother called down and asked us if we wanted some hot chocolate.

I must admit that although these incidents were all very nice, they were, nevertheless, beginning to bother hell out of me, too. I sure didn't want to be tied down at the age of fourteen, but then pride made me keep charging ahead. The guys used to kid me all the time about BB, and ask me if I was getting any, so naturally I always said that I was getting plenty and they actually believed me, I think. Anyway, later on in the spring, after many frenzied sorties in the balcony of the Rialto Theater, BB and I sat on her porch swing one Friday night and started fooling around real good. In a little while, I was holding onto her knocker for dear life, and then —just a little later—she reached down and touched me. I liked to jump right up out of the swing at first, but then—when I got used to the idea—everything was a bit of all right. She started to fumble with my fly, and then whispered to me: "Take him out for me," and I was going to only BB's mother called down from upstairs that it was time for BB to come in. So BB went in and I buttoned up my fly.

I was so shook up that I missed the last bus, so I had to walk all the way home from the Gardens. I didn't get back until nearly two. No one was waiting up for me, and I was glad about that, but I knew I'd hear about it—which I did the very next morning. Both Mom and Dad asked me what time I had gotten in, so I told them the truth for a change and said that the lousy bus had gone and passed right by me and so I had to walk home 'cause that had been the last bus. Well, it wasn't the complete truth, but it was close enough because my Mom got passed up by that bus many times and knew how it felt.

Chuck wasn't fooled, though. He took me outside afterward and said that he better tell me something about the birds and the bees, but I told him I already knew about that stuff, and then he got mad and pushed me behind the garage and tried to beat me up, only he never could. "What do you mean, you already know?" he yelled at me. "*I* didn't know until last year!" But then we talked things over, and I appreciated it and was glad he did talk things over with me, 'cause even though I said I knew everything, I didn't really know much at all, and I don't think any of the guys I hung around with did, except maybe Doug Dickey who was just about crazy.

I didn't go out with BB much after that time on her porch. I was scared that her mother would catch us doing something, and besides, I went away to camp for the summer anyway and knew that things would peter out on their own. The next fall, BB started dating high school seniors and I got all wound up in football. When I was a senior, BB and I went the full route in the back of my old man's car eleven times in the Tamaques Park parking lot, and even though it was very awkward, it was also very nice. But my first actual time was one summer up at camp when I was sixteen, but I never told BB that because I think it might have upset her, she attaching a great deal of importance to such things.

So, my old man and I talked at the Polo Grounds. First of all he wanted to know why I wanted to join the Army. I told him I just didn't want to stay in school.

"That's foolish," he replied. "Foolish!"

I looked out at the field. The Giants were at bat again but my old man was hardly even paying attention to the game. I think that sort of impressed me. "It may be foolish," I stated, watching Wes Westrum pop out to Billy Cox. "But it's even more foolish to stay in college when I'm not really doing anything there."

Dad nodded. "You may think you're not doing anything, but really you're doing quite a bit. Classes have hardly started, and besides, how many freshmen make the Ohio State varsity?"

"I haven't made it yet," I said. "And the classes I'm taking are stupid." They were, too.

"That's not the point."

"Well, what is the point then?"

I don't know why I was getting so angry—probably because I knew Dad was right.

"ROTC is important," Dad said.

"I don't want to be an officer."

"That's ridiculous," he scoffed. "Why be a private when you can be an officer?"

"Because I want to be a private," I said. "Chuck was a private."

Dad looked back out at the field. The game was in the fourth inning. Still one-zip, Dodgers. There was a lot of tension in the Polo Grounds and not all of it was concerned with the outcome of the game. All of a sudden, I felt pretty foolish, pretty guilty, sitting there in a ball park while Chuck's ashes were six feet under in Montclair, New Jersey, or Korea, or someplace. I felt ashamed about a lot of things.

The closest I had ever come to feeling that ashamed with my old man was back when I had been eight, and Chuck thirteen. Dad had said that Chuck couldn't go to some Boy Scout meeting and Chuck was really furious about it. It was one of the few times I had ever seen Chuck really mad. Usually, he never seemed to get mad about anything. So I followed him out to our hut in the backyard and after a while we played war, and things like that, but I could tell that his heart was not in the defense of the Maginot Line. Suddenly he turned to me. "Private," he barked.

"Yessir," I replied.

"Private, go in there and tell Dad he's full of shit."

Well, when I was eight years old I didn't know what I know now, and so naturally I followed my older brother's instructions to the letter. It was a Saturday morning, I recall, and I can remember marching into the house in full military regalia (meaning I had my uncle's captured World War I helmet on my head and a six-shooter in my fist) and I found Dad and Old Man Ewart in the living room discussing the next War Bond Drive. They laughed when they saw me, but they didn't laugh very long. I looked Dad right in the eye. "Chuck told me to tell you that you're full of shit," I said.

I didn't salute or anything afterward, I just ran out of the house as quickly as I could. Somehow I realized right away that maybe, just maybe, I had done something I shouldn't have done. When I got back to the hut, Chuck looked at me anxiously.

"What did you do?" he asked.

"What you told me to do."

"You *didn't*. Everything?"

"Everything."

"Oh boy," Chuck whined, starting to cry. "What did you do that for?"

"You told me to," I answered, also starting to cry.

"Oh boy!" Chuck shook his head. "Who did you say it to?"

"Dad. Old Man Ewart. And Mom heard me, too."

"*Oh boy!*" he cried. I'd never seen Chuck so scared. It wasn't like him at all. Suddenly he stood up and put his Boy Scout hat on, then grabbed his canteen. "Come on," he announced. "We're going on a hike."

"Where to?"

"I don't know where to," he answered, "but we're not coming back."

So we hiked and hiked and hiked. Then, when it started to get dark, we decided that we better hike back and spend the night in our hut. When we snuck back into the yard, tired and hungry, Chuck whispered to me that after this, whenever someone told me to do something foolish, no matter how old he was, that I shouldn't do it no matter what.

"Did you tell me to do something foolish?" I asked.

"Yes," he replied seriously. "Yes, I sure did."

But I didn't believe him, 'cause Chuck didn't go around telling people to do foolish things. Especially his own little brother.

After a while, Dad came out and told us to get inside the house and eat some dinner. We didn't say anything, but I was sort of glad because I was sure getting hungry. When we walked into the dining room we were both scared, but we managed to sit down at the table anyway. It was really weird. Usually, everyone'd be talking a blue streak, but there was only dead silence this time. I really started to feel pretty foolish and ashamed. I guessed that's how my Dad wanted us to feel.

And there I was at the Polo Grounds, also feeling pretty foolish, ashamed, and funny. What difference did it make if I wanted to go into the Army or not? It made a lot of difference and I knew it.

And so did my old man. He just wouldn't stop bugging me on the subject, though. "You know," he said, "as long as this police action is going on over there it would really be stupid to join the Army. Why go looking for trouble?"

I didn't answer him; I was just feeling too foolish. There we were, surrounded by baseball fans going crazy about the game while we argued about going into the Army. The people next to us must have thought we were really nuts. So I leaned forward and studied the game as if I really gave a damn. Everything—the whole pennant race—was riding on this one game, but I couldn't really have cared less. Even with all the tension in the air.

The Dodger fans stood up at the top of the seventh and I joined them. When the Dodgers were retired, my Dad looked over at me, smiled, and then stood up for his stretch. Big deal. Did anyone really care?

The Giants seemed to care. Monte Irvin came up and doubled off the wall in left. The noise around us got a little louder. Some fans started to clap in unison. "This might be it," someone called out. "This might be it!"

Whitey Lockman squared away to bunt at the ball. Hodges charged down from first . . . but it was a ball.

"He should hit away," my old man said. "Leo's playing it too conservative."

What do you know? I thought.

Newcombe stretched, checked Irvin at second, then fired in to the plate. Lockman laid down a perfect bunt along the third-base line. Rube Walker had a little trouble getting to the ball, but it didn't make any difference: Lockman was already on first, and Irvin beat the throw to third. My Dad was on his feet, his fist raised up in the air. He looked around and grinned at the rest of the Giant fans in our area. Then he looked across at the plate and started to shake his head. "That bonehead," he mumbled, gesturing toward home as he sat down. "Watch him hit into a double play." My old man always had a lot of confidence in his team. Bobby Thomson took two called strikes, then fouled off two pitches. Finally, he connected and the ball sailed out high and far, but straightaway to dead center. The Duke retreated a few steps and gathered it in. Irvin scored easily from third and the fans roared their belated approval. The score was now one to one. All tied up. Tension all over the place now.

I was used to tension. I don't mean being a spectator at baseball games, no matter how important the game was. I mean after playing two and a half years for the Northwood Bulldogs I found out what real tension was like—not any of this phony professional crap. When you're a professional that's what you're paid to do, right? But when you're only sixteen and seventeen years old, why it's a little bit different. Especially when you play in front of sold-out crowds week after week; when all anyone talks about downtown is the coming big game; when that's all you've thought about all your life. Needless to say, Northwood was a football-crazy town and Crazy Ed Ringen was an absolute madman of a coach.

The Booster Club once had a big campaign to change Crazy Ed's image in town. They wanted everyone to start calling him Kicking Ed, but the idea never really caught on. Ed was crazy on Saturday afternoons and that's all there was to it. He used to walk up and down the sidelines during a game spitting between his teeth like anything, and then, after each play, no matter if there had been a gain or a loss, he'd wind up and kick at the turf. Kicking Ed Ringen—no, somehow it just never caught on.

Crazy Ed had a fabulous record in Northwood and we'd been State Champions several times. I grew up dreaming about playing for Crazy Ed someday and there wasn't a moment in my childhood that wasn't directed toward that eventuality. By the time I was in junior high, I knew all of the Northwood plays and, thanks to Ed's scouting system, he knew quite a bit about me, too. We didn't have the Little League or any of that crap in those days, but Ed found out about all potential football players in town, and sometimes the surrounding communities as well, and he never had any serious trouble getting candidates for The Team. Some kids grow up wanting to play shortstop for the Yankees or Dodgers, but in Northwood you grew up wanting to play for Crazy Ed's varsity. College, and professional, football were for the middle-aged, pot-bellied set; the real goal was to play against Plainfield in the traditional Turkey Day Classic before 12,000 rabid fans. Nothing else really mattered.

There was a lot of pressure on us during football season, but we expected that sort of thing so it didn't bother us all that much. I mean that was part of the game, wasn't it? But that 1950 season was really a rough one, pressure-wise, even if we did wind up going undefeated. South River tied us on a lousy sleeper play in the final three minutes, but that was the only close game we played all year—until the Plainfield game. Crazy Ed was pretty calm and collected whenever we had a losing game (only two in my high school career), but I can't say the same for our friends, The Downtown Boosters. They expected us to win each week, just like clockwork, so that when we were upset—or just plain lousy—why, it came as a big surprise to them. They didn't realize how lucky we were a lot of the time. I mean Crazy Ed was a good coach, even if he was a little eccentric. One Downtown Booster wouldn't even let us come into his lousy ice cream store after we lost a game. It didn't bother us at the time, but the next week, after whipping Union, 45–6, we snuck into this jerk's back room and peed into his vanilla ice cream vat. One time, during the '49 season, we lost to Columbia and were picked up by the cops afterward. They were really nasty to us—for no reason at all—and told us we better not lose any more games that year. We didn't lose any more, but it wasn't because of the stupid cops.

But because we were tied with Plainfield for State honors my senior year, the pressure mounted all season long. That early tie with South River didn't help matters on any, either. The week before the Turkey Day Classic was really something. Every time one of the guys went downtown he'd be bugged by one of the Boosters. They kept asking us how we were going to do Thursday morning. What did they expect us to say, that we thought we'd lose or something? To tell the truth, I wasn't all that sure how we were going to do. I mean we kept shouting that no one was going to whip us—and there were pep rallies every day—but I still wasn't so sure. We had been lucky to beat Plainfield the year before, and this year Wilt Randall was breaking all sorts of records for them. It was going to be a close game, that's all I knew.

Mr. Jenkins at the stationery store downtown called me aside a day or two before the game and whispered some advice to me. "Break that nigger's leg," he suggested. "Without him, they're nothing."

I didn't even bother answering the idiot. I should have said something to him, but Crazy Ed had warned us about being snotty to any of the Boosters. Our town was full of spies, and gossips, and middle-aged bastards who thought that football was both the beginning and the end. Well, football was important to us, but I never really understood why grown-ups always took it so seriously—we were the ones who were playing, not Them.

I must say my parents were pretty good about the pressures of football season. My mother never really talked about football except to ask if anyone got hurt in the games. If no one got hurt then it was a good game as far as she was concerned. She'd gone to two or three games my sophomore year, but she got all excited when I went into the game and carried the ball, so she simply stopped going. She'd hang around the house on Saturday afternoons waiting to hear all the car horns honking after a Northwood victory. My old man was especially big on honking horns after a winning game. But I will say this—he never bugged me about football during the season. He was a Booster, sure, and he may have been as bad as all the rest of them, but at least at home he left me alone, and I was glad about that, believe me.

Anyway, against Plainfield, we went the entire first half without a score. Both sides had been nervous and neither of us had mounted any real drives. When the whistle blew, ending the half, I could tell that the fans were starting to get nervous, too. Why should they be nervous—hadn't they all prayed for victory?

In the locker room between halves, I thought Crazy Ed was really going to let us have it like he sometimes did, but he didn't. He came over to just about everyone on the first team and told us quietly that we were all playing good ball, and that we shouldn't worry about anything—the second half would take care of itself, he said, and that we should just go out there on the field and have some fun. Then he outlined some defenses we could use against Wilt Randall, in case he got rambunctious, and then—just before we were to go back out onto the field—he turned to us and stared down at the concrete floor silently. We waited for him to say something, anxious to get back outside, but he still kept staring down at the floor. Finally, he slowly looked up and we could all see that he was crying. "Boys," he mumbled. "You're the best team this school has ever had. . . ." He started to say something else, but then abruptly turned around and walked out onto the field.

At first we didn't know what to do. And then we did—we were going to go out there and win that stupid game for Crazy Ed and nothing was going to stop us. We knew Ed was probably just putting on an act for us, but we didn't care. We weren't going to worry about all those idiots in the stands, or the Boosters, or anyone. All we had to worry about was winning that Turkey Day Classic for Crazy Ed Ringen.

And we stomped all over Plainfield in the second half. It might not have looked that way from the stands, but we knew we were stomping them. Wilt Randall wasn't able to do anything that half, and even though we only managed to score once, we must have held onto the ball almost three-fourths of the half. I plunged over from the three halfway through the third period, and Bobby White added the point. We almost scored two more times, but one was called back on a penalty and the other time we just missed.

When the final whistle blew, we carried Crazy Ed off the field. While we were waiting for the bus to come up to the locker room, the Plainfield team walked slowly past us. I saw Wilt Randall and he smiled at me, but then I heard some of the stupid Plainfield Boosters shouting at him and he stopped smiling. I guess their Boosters were just as bad as our Boosters—all they wanted you to do was win.

Going back to Northwood in the bus, Bobby White was sick, and several of the other guys threw up, too. I was sitting by the window, but I was almost sick myself. I wonder if anyone would have understood—instead of whooping it up and hollering like crazy, most of our State Championship team was busy being sick all over themselves.

Tension? Yes, we knew all about tension.

•

And so did the Giants. In the top of the eighth, Reese and Snider both singled. Then Maglie broke off a curve that bounced in the dirt and kicked past Westrum. Reese scored from third with the tie-breaking run. Oh, brother, everyone in the lousy Polo Grounds was yelling something. Everyone except my old man. Then the Giants decided to walk Jackie and I hooted some myself at that. OK, men on first and second . . . Andy Pafko at bat. He swung and smashed the ball off Bobby Thomson's glove, Snider scoring from second and Jackie dashing all the way around to third.

"That Thomson!" my old man growled, writing it all down in his scorecard.

"Take him out," someone else shouted.

"Kee-rist!"

But the Dodger fans were happy. Very happy. "More," they chanted. "More, more, more!"

After Hodges went out, Billy Cox came up and hit another ball past Thomson at third and one more run came in. My old man threw down his scorecard with disgust. He was really all worked up. He looked over at me and shook his head. "That Thomson isn't a third baseman," he grumbled. "He never was."

Why didn't he shut up? Why couldn't he just accept the fact that the Giants were going to lose? Why did he have to second-guess everything? Why didn't he keep his mouth shut like he usually did at ball games?

Hell, the Dodgers were going to win; everyone could see that. And after they won, I was going to quit school and join the Army.

It was all settled.

3

I think if Dad had known what I had decided, he wouldn't have let me go ahead and do it. He was excited about the game, sure, but he also didn't want me in the Army. I knew that much, all right.

But I was mad enough to go ahead. Confused enough, too. And the idea of fans yelling at the players, and second-guessing everything really bugged me. What did they think, that they weren't trying their hardest? Jesus!

Of course, I never really tried at OSU—not at first, anyway. I don't know why, but I never got into the swing of things there my freshman year. I knew I was going to have to learn all about the T-formation and a whole new system, but I wasn't really prepared for some of Smokey's ways, nor for the ways of Columbus, Ohio, either. They were certainly crazy over football out there, but they didn't hesitate to criticize the team, or the coaches, or anything. The students seemed to be all right, but the only students I really knew were connected with the team.

I was in good shape, though, and I didn't mind the emphasis on the physical contact. What I did mind was having so doggone many guys ahead of me. The fact that I didn't know anyone out there at first didn't bother me at all, but I did have trouble understanding what everyone was talking about. They said things like "waiting on" when they meant "waiting for" and all the upper classmen talked about was their old coach who had quit, and about Smokey. There was a lot of speculation as to what kind of coach Smokey was going to be, but as far as I could tell, Smokey was all business and reasonably fair. I knew that 'cause that's what everyone went around saying—Smokey's tough, but fair.

I had an athletic scholarship, of course, but it didn't mean all that much 'cause everyone on the team seemed to have some sort of scholarship. My marks hadn't been so red-hot in high school, but I hadn't flunked anything and I had made All-County fullback in both the Elizabeth *Daily Journal* and the Plainfield *Courier*. Actually, I was pretty good in math and really liked solid geometry and trigonometry, and stuff like that, and I was even sort of thinking about majoring in math, but after those first few weeks of two-a-day practice sessions I knew that if I stayed on the team I'd have to major in the easiest subject there was, if I was forced to major in anything.

I wasn't all that excited about living in a dormitory with most of the rest of the jocks, either, but I didn't have much choice in the matter. My roommate was a guy named Hubert Honachyevski from outside of Cleveland and we got along real well, mainly because we hardly said anything to each other. He was also a fullback, but every time he was given the ball in practice drills, he fumbled it right up. That was Hubert's problem. My problem was the cotton-picking T-formation. I just couldn't get used to it at first. I should have had more patience with myself, 'cause I knew they didn't expect too much from freshmen, but I still wanted to be in a position to score some points for the big scarlet and gray team.

But I let my impatience show, I think. Or maybe it was this guy, Ray Lind, who bugged me right from the time he found out I came from New Jersey. I don't know what he had against New Jersey, exactly, except for the fact that it was close to New York City. Anyway, he bugged me every chance he got, and after a while I started to bug him right back. Hubert told me one night that I shouldn't go around sassing seniors, but I just couldn't stop myself, and whenever

Ray Lind bugged me about New York-New Jersey I bugged him right back about Piqua, Ohio.

After practice one evening, Ray Lind snapped his towel at me coming out of the shower, and since I wasn't in such a red-hot mood at the time, I started right for him. However, I was stopped by about five or six guys on the varsity before either of us could do any damage. It was just as well; I didn't want to get into any fights—especially not with someone on the first team. But after that incident, Ray Lind didn't bug me as much, but we never became what you might call bosom buddies.

It was a little better when classes started—we only had to practice once a day then. A lot of the upper classmen practiced almost all day, but they were majoring in phys ed or something and the extra practice was just part of some special seminar, I think. They wouldn't let me take any math that first semester, and it was probably just as well. They did let me take ROTC, though, which was a big joke because none of the guys on the team had to show up for drills or anything.

During the second week of classes, I got Dad's first call about Chuck. Somehow the news just didn't seem real. I told Hubert about it, one noontime when we were killing time on the Oval, but since it didn't seem to affect me any, it didn't affect him either.

A day or so later, I was called into the coach's office—and I thought for a while that I was going to be cut from the team. But I wasn't cut, the freshman coordinator told me they were going to convert me to guard. He asked me what I thought of the idea.

I said that I didn't think very highly of that idea because I had never even considered playing in the line.

"Well," he said. "You better think highly of it, 'cause that's where you're gonna be."

The next few days of practice were pure hell. The rest of the team was getting ready for the SMU game, but I was being given a kindergarten course in football. I learned how to block. I learned how to hit dummies. I learned how to pull out. I learned how to really hustle. There were about ten of us in this special unit, Hubert included. All of us had been backs in high school, too. At night, my roommate and I talked about quitting the team, but we weren't serious—Hubert didn't want to end up in a steel mill like his brothers had, and I didn't want to go back to New Jersey.

But a few days later I got the second call from Dad and decided, what the hell, why not go back to New Jersey?

"We still have three outs," Dad said hopefully. "Dark, Mueller, and Monte Irvin coming to bat. Could be worse. Could be worse."

Four to one, last of the ninth, how the hell could it be any worse? The Giants had come a long way—from thirteen and a half games back—but the momentum had changed. Robby, Reese, the Duke, Hodges—those guys weren't about to blow a 4–1 lead in the last inning. No way. I still felt a little funny about what I had decided to do, but that's the way it was going to be.

It reminded me of how I felt the time Dad had tried to teach me how to drive. He got all flustered and nervous when I didn't do exactly what he told me, which made me even more nervous and flustered. I'm glad I didn't have to learn about football from my Dad; he never was able to teach me very much. Every time he tried to, both of us would end up getting all excited. Actually, Chuck ended up teaching me how to drive. I don't know why Dad couldn't have been as patient as Chuck was with me, but he sure wasn't. At least, not when it came to teaching me how to drive.

But Chuck was dead.

And my old man was sitting right next to me.

Alvin Dark walked up to the plate. I had liked him when he and Stanky had played for the Braves, but once he went to the Giants—well, that was that. That little Stanky had been a favorite of mine, too, especially when he had played for the Bums. Oh, those old Giants had really been fun to hate when they were just big and fat and all they could do was hit home runs. But then they got Leo, and that made them a little harder to hate 'cause Leo was really a Dodger. And then came Dark and Stanky . . .

And there was Alvin Dark, looking out at Big Newk . . . big number 36. Newk was still humming that ball in there. With a little luck he could sew up the pennant with only three pitches. With a little luck. But Newk was never especially lucky. I remember once how he lost a game in the '49 World Series on a cheap homer by Tommy Henrich in the bottom of the ninth. God, I really used to hate the Yankees. Anyone with any real sense couldn't help but hate the Yankees. All they ever did was win.

Dark took two quick strikes from Newcombe, then dug in again at the plate, waving that dark-colored bat of his back and forth, back and forth. I could see the players in both dugouts moving around nervously, clapping their hands together, staring out at the field. Dark stared out at Newk and swung at the third pitch. I could tell it was going to be a hit as soon as it left the bat. I could sense it. Dark had always been a good right-field hitter, a great hit-and-run man—and there the ball was, bouncing off Hodges' glove into right field. Base hit.

Man on first, no one out. My Dad was getting as nervous as everyone else around us. There wasn't as much noise as there had been at the start of the game, but then everyone knew that this was going to be it. The shit was approaching the fan and it didn't do any good to make any noise until you could see which way it was going to fly.

Don (Mandrake) Mueller strolled casually up to the plate. He walked back to the batter's resin bag for a moment and said a few words to Monte Irvin, then returned to the batter's box and touched the edge of home plate with his bat. Dad edged up in his seat. I could tell he was getting all tense inside, just like when he was trying to teach me how to drive. Newcombe checked Dark at first, then scowled down at Mueller. Rube Walker pounded his big glove and squatted behind the plate. Newk checked Dark again, then stretched.

Make him hit it on the ground, I urged silently. Make him hit it to Jackie. Sure: Jackie to Reese to Hodges, just like that. That's what we wanted, a grounder to second.

But Newk was tired. I knew he must be tired. Carl Erskine and Ralph Branca were warming up in the Dodger bullpen right below us. Get Erskine in there, I thought. Get Erskine in there right now.

Mueller swung on the next pitch, though, and belted it cleanly between first and second. Suddenly, everyone was on his feet—making noise. My old man's fist was raised high up into the air—where else? Dark sped around to third as the throw from Furillo came into Reese, holding Mueller at first.

OK, so what? The Giants were still three runs behind and a double play would kill the rally, right? Who was up? Monte Irvin. He hit into a lot of double plays. Sure give them a run, make it exciting—but get that double play.

My old man returned to his seat and scribbled into his scorecard. "Tying run's at the plate," he said to me, smiling in a sickly sort of way. Giant fans were never too optimistic.

"Quick triple play," I predicted.

He looked at me with surprise, but didn't answer.

Walker talked to Big Newk for a few moments, then trotted back behind the plate. Newk stretched, checked the runners, then fired. Monte Irvin swung and there was a huge cheer as the ball left the bat. But then the cheers turned into groans as the ball sailed almost straight up into the air. Jackie pointed it out, and Hodges drifted into foul territory and took the high pop-up. One out. One big out. A double play now would end the game.

"Darn," my old man said, sitting down impatiently. "A long fly," he whispered. "That's all we need—a long fly."

They needed more than that. I think my old man really thought that Irvin hadn't been trying to hit a long fly, or a homer, or anything. Didn't he realize that those guys were busting their balls to win? Hell, Irvin should have tried for a single, not the big one—even with that short left-field fence. 'Cause now we had the Jints where we wanted them.

I watched Lockman walk up to the plate, then look down at Leo at third as he knocked some dirt out of his spikes. The fourth man up in the inning already. With a little luck it could have been over.

But it wasn't over.

A lot of things never work out exactly as you plan them. I have a bad habit of trying to anticipate how everything is going to turn out. Like going out to Columbus on the train, I spent a whole lot of time speculating on how I was going to make it in Big Ten football. I mean I had to spend twelve hours on the lousy Pennsy, what else was I going to do? I knew I might have a little trouble making the varsity, especially my freshman year, but that didn't stop me from thinking about scoring the winning touchdown against Michigan in the final two seconds of play. I sure didn't daydream about not making the team, or fumbling during a key play, or something like that. I mean if you're going to daydream you might as well win the big game in the last few seconds, right?

I knew there had to be both winners and losers, but I never really gave losing much thought. In all the sports books I'd ever read, why very few heroes ever lost the game in the last few seconds of play. I really liked all those John R. Tunis books, even if they were about Ivy League stuff a lot of the time. I think I read every one of them as a kid. All those spikes going clickety-click—clickety-clack . . . *The Kid from Tompkinsville . . . The World Series . . . The Iron Duke. . . .* Man, they were all pretty good. The trouble with those books, though, is that they're always about Big Games, or Good Clean Kids, or winning in the last few seconds. They rarely mention anything about the sweaty, stinking, rotten socks and jocks; the horseshit of the locker room; the injuries and the fights.

But I had good, clean thoughts about State, 'cause there was absolutely no sense in having bad thoughts. And if I knew that the coach was going to convert me into an offensive guard, I would have gotten off that train in Altoona sure as shooting.

Lockman stepped up to the plate. Big Newk was really looking tired now, even from where we were sitting. Men on first and third, one out. A double play would end it, but Lockman was a hard man to double up.

Dad had his scorecard rolled up and was hitting it into his left hand. I leaned forward and stared as hard as I could across the field, trying to put the whammy on Lockman. Hit it on the ground, I urged, but right at somebody.

Newcombe checked the runners, then heaved the ball in toward the plate. Lockman took ball one, then looked down to Leo again. Rube Walker squatted back down behind the batter and, once again, Big Newk aimed the ball in to the plate. The pitch was on the outside corner and Lockman swung late, slapping down at it. The ball sliced sharply past Cox at third, then rolled into the left-field corner. Oh, how many times had I seen Lockman do that—slash a double over third. Jesus!

Everyone yelled at once when the ball had been signaled fair. Dark raced home easily while Pafko hurried over for the ball. Reese ran out into left for the relay while Cox picked himself up and scrambled back to cover third. Mueller streaked in to the base, then started to slide. I could tell something was wrong as he sort of turned over as he slid. But he still managed to beat the throw—and Lockman beat the relay to second.

We all stood up and looked over at Mueller, writhing on the ground by third. Leo and Cox bent over him, then the trainer ran over from the dugout. You could feel the excitement in the stands, but there still wasn't too much noise.

"What happened?" Dad asked.

"He caught his spikes," I replied. You could see that Mueller was in pain and they had to bring out a stretcher and carry him off. While he was being taken out the applause started and then roared up to a crescendo. It was as if everyone finally realized that this was really it. The score was 4 to 2, now, and the winning run was coming to the plate.

"Oh, no," Dad mumbled, looking at his scorecard. "That bum Thomson's up again." He shook his head, then looked over at me. "Maybe they'll walk him to get a force at any base. Yeah, that kid Mays is up next—they'll walk Thomson to get at the kid."

I looked across the field, thinking. They wouldn't put the winning run on base. A single would tie the game up and put the winning run at third. But Thomson had already singled once and had knocked in the only Giant run up until that inning. Oh, what the hell, Charley, I thought. Maybe he is a bum, walk him like my old man wants. Forget about the percentages. Let it all ride or fall with the kid, Mays.

Charley Dressen walked out to the mound, then patted Big Newk on the back. Rube, Reese and Jackie were already there; Hodges and Cox just a few steps away. Both Erskine and Branca were still firing hard in the bullpen, and Charley signaled for Branca. Number 13 picked up his jacket and slowly walked in to the mound. Duke said something to him as he trudged by. Newk plopped the ball into Branca's glove, patted him on the back, then slowly walked away. The manager stayed at the mound, watching the warm-up pitches, then followed Newk into the dugout.

Clint Hartung came in to run for Mueller and Leo whispered something to him. Hartung nodded, then stood cautiously on top of third base. Pee Wee shouted something over to Jackie, then stared in to the plate. Branca leaned down for his sign from Walker.

Everything was all set. Score: 4 to 2, Dodgers. Bobby Thomson at the plate. Lockman on second, Hartung on third. One out.

Thomson adjusted his feet in the batter's box, then his elbows. Dad was unable to sit still. He stood, then sat, then stood up again. His scorecard was rolled up tightly in his right fist.

Branca was all set for his first pitch to Thomson.

All of a sudden I felt sick.

I'm not exactly sure why I felt sick.

I guess I was still a little shook up about Chuck, and even though I hadn't shown it, it was bothering me a whole lot. It just didn't seem possible that I'd never see him again. He had no business being in the Army in the first place. He didn't believe in war or any of that stuff, only science. He should never have joined up. They should have taken someone like me, instead. At least I knew how to play the fuckin' game.

Sure, I was the one who knew how to play at being John Wayne.

Jackie bluffed Lockman back to second, then looked in toward the batter. Branca fired. The ball sailed right down the pipe. Strike one, Jorda indicated quickly. Thomson looked like he had been hypnotized. "C'mon, you big bum," my old man shouted. "Hit it!" Lockman walked back to second and touched the bag with his foot, then shouted something in to the batter. Maybe it was encouragement; maybe it was just to bug his teammate for not hitting at that good pitch. That's all Thomson needed right then—more people bugging him at a time like that.

I looked into the dugouts and saw all the players looking out at the field. Why was I feeling sorry for Thomson? Heck, I wanted the big dummy to strike out or, better yet, hit into a quick double play. But somehow I felt sorry for him being up there at a time like that.

"Oh, I wish they'd walk that bum," my old man growled.

I started to grumble something back, but changed my mind. What good would it do? Just don't give him anything good to hit, Ralph. Make him go for a bad pitch, or walk him. I looked at the kid, Willie Mays, in the on-deck circle, holding onto a couple of bats. What a spot for a kid to be in. If Thomson did walk, he'd be up with the bases loaded. Willie-fuckin'-Mays!

But Thomson was still at bat, digging in for the next pitch. My old man leaned in toward the plate, shaking just a little. It was the first time I could ever remember seeing Dad get excited at a game. "C'mon," he whispered. "C'mon."

Branca leaned in again, caught the sign, then checked the runners and fired. The ball sailed in, high and tight. It looked for a second that it might hit Thomson's elbow—that he'd have to duck—but just at the last moment he whipped his bat around and connected with the ball.

There was a sudden, loud gasp. Thomson looked up. The ball started to twist toward us. It was hard to tell just how hard it was hit. Snider came over to his right, and Pafko started to take a few choppy steps to his left. For a second, I thought that Andy was going to have a chance for it, or at least play it off the wall. . . . Then there was an explosion of noise. Solid noise.

Oh no, I thought. It can't be. It wasn't hit that hard at all. My stomach growled and I felt hollow and dizzy. Why didn't everyone shut up, I thought. Why was everyone making so much noise?

The ball hardly even arched at all. It came on a twisting line out to us and landed just a section away. Oh, sweet son of a bitch.

"Cheap!" I shouted out. "Cheap!"

But no one heard me. No one paid the least bit of attention to me. Absolutely every single person in the Polo Grounds was on his feet, shouting, crying, jumping up and down . . . something. But I sat down. I just sat down and listened to all the lousy noise.

My Dad jumped up and down, up and down. He pounded a neighbor on the back. "Oh-ho," he shouted. "Oh-ho!" He waved his arms in the air. "I don't believe it!" he cried. "I don't believe it."

You just saw it, you better believe it.

"The Giants won the pennant," someone called. "The Giants won the pennant!"

"Bobby Thomson!"

"Oh, what a beautiful bum!"

That bum, Bobby Thomson.

Winning the pennant for the Giants, just like that. I didn't believe it. I didn't want to believe it. I tried to tell myself I didn't care, but I knew I did care.

I stood up and watched the pandemonium. All of a sudden, everyone seemed to be a Giant fan. People were running onto the field . . . people were screaming . . . paper was blowing all over the place . . .

The players were excited, too . . . Leo and Stanky were rolling around on the ground by third . . . Thomson was being mobbed . . .

And the Bums . . . the Bums were trudging slowly, painfully across the outfield to their clubhouse. They couldn't seem to believe it, either.

I sat back down. My old man was still waving his arms

around, shouting in chorus with all the others. He even ripped his scorecard up and threw the pieces into the air.

The Giants had won the pennant!

Suddenly, he stopped shouting and looked down at me. "I don't believe it," he announced.

"Who cares?" I mumbled.

He hit me on the shoulder. "Can't take it, huh, Pete?"

Oh, kiss my ass, I murmured, but he didn't hear me. You *are* full of shit, you know that?

Then Dad sat back down and took ahold of my arm. I thought for a second that he'd heard me, but he hadn't.

"I'm sorry," he said quietly. "I'm sorry the Dodgers lost, Pete."

I didn't say anything. But I could feel him looking at me. "School's the best thing," he whispered.

I still looked straight ahead.

"Please go back to school," he urged.

The crowd around us was still going absolutely crazy. The noise was fantastic.

I turned to him. "What?" I asked. I was going to ask something else, but I didn't. There was just too much noise.

So I looked back at the field—at all the people shouting, jumping, screaming—doing something.

My old man and I sat there quietly.

"I don't want you in the Army," he said, his voice sounding sort of funny. I don't want to lose you, too . . . I . . ." He stopped and leaned forward in his seat and stared straight ahead. I shook my head, not knowing what to do. Then, without even thinking about it, I reached over and held onto Dad's arm. I thought he might cry—I know I felt sort of like crying myself. But neither of us did.

So I just held onto him.

And the crowd roared on. They yelled—they screamed. They mobbed the clubhouse steps calling for Thomson. They still couldn't believe it.

But my Dad and I believed it. We didn't have to pay any attention at all to the bedlam on the field to believe it. We just held onto each other and knew.

So I went back to State. And played some more football.

I have often wondered what would have happened if Charley Dressen had told Branca to walk Bobby Thomson.

PART TWO

The Kid Comes Back

(1956)

1

I stood by the fence feeling the cold, wet, clammy rain dribble down my neck. I stood by that miserable perimeter fence looking over at Dependent Building 8905.

I knew Dependent Building 8905 all right. I knew that building from top to bottom. A lot of the guys used to kid me about sneaking down behind the R & U shack to stand by the perimeter fence. They sure would have been shook up if they'd known the real truth, but no one really wants to know the real truth. It was cold all right, though. Cold and miserable. Good old Deutschland. That's what that fat sergeant had called it back in Frankfurt at the repple-depple. "Good old Deutschland." Oh, I just loved those resonant, overfed sergeants. SFC Justice Y. Baldini, that's who it was. I remember him looking us up and down, up and down in the courtyard of that repple-depple.

"Young gentlemuns," he called out in that mellow, basso-profundo voice of his. "It can be did." He gestured in the general direction of the street. "Now, you see them fancy-looking frauleins over there? Young gentlemuns, I am going to give each and every one of you a pass in five or seven minutes so you can raus down to the PX for some chow. But first, I'm taking some of my own time to give you young troopers a piece of advice. I said *advice*. . . ." He looked at us for a few seconds, his beady little eyes flashing from one end of the formation to the other. "Now," he went on. "Let me draw you a mental picture of the situation. The very romantic area to your immediate right is known as Five Mark Park. Do not confuse this area with WAC Circle which is where the PX is. Do you know how much five marks is, young gentlemuns? Five marks is one dollar and twenty-five cents. One dollar and twenty-five cents." He paused for a moment to let this grand sum have its effect, then continued. "For a buck and two bits you can jump behind a bush of Five Mark Park with one of them fancy-looking frauleins over there and have yourselves a ball, don't that sound sort of romantic?"

One of the guys in the formation started to laugh. SFC Baldini stopped his resonant lecture and looked at the private. "Don't laugh, young trooper, it can very well be did. Them fancy-looking frauleins will be glad to oblige each and every one of you for only five marks." All of a sudden he took one quick step forward. "And if I catches any swinging dick in Five Mark Park I'm gonna have his tail, 'cause as sure as I'm standing here on my own time to tell you this you're gonna end up on sick call." He stopped and looked again at the soldier who had laughed. "So, go ahead," he bellowed. "Give that ever-loving pecker of yours a treat, that's what the taxpayers of our great country sent you over here for, wasn't it—to give those peckers of yours a treat? Yessir. Yes, *sir*. You young troopers has got it made. Uncle Sam sends you over here so you can jump right into Five Mark Park and have yourselves a treat. Now, some people may say it's no worse than the common fuckin' cold, but let me say onto you it *is* worse than the common fuckin' cold. And believe you me, young gentlemuns, the treatment we got over here does smart. Yes, huh uh, it surely does smart." He snapped his heels together and looked straight ahead. "Move out for chow," he roared.

A few minutes later we were out on the street, walking down to the PX. The frauleins approached us, as promised, but at that time we were all thinking more of the treatment than we were of the treat. We were also hungry.

•

And there I was, by that miserable fence again. "C'mon, Steph," I whispered. "C'mon out here." I walked back to the R & U shack and leaned up against it, not taking my eyes off Dependent Building 8905. Especially the third window from the left, second floor. "C'mon, Steph, you son of a bitch, c'mon out here."

Fifteen more hours of this crap, I thought. Just fifteen more hours of this crap and then I'd go on leave and it would all be over. But God it was cold. God it was wet. I pulled up the collar of my field jacket and stomped my feet on the wet, cold, mushy ground. Old Lou'd have my tail if he caught me wearing a field jacket over my civvies. Old Lou see me and he'd have my tail anyway. Well, what did he expect? What did he expect when he married a chick from his hometown who didn't really love him? No one marries a chick from his hometown anyway, especially when she doesn't even love him.

So there I was, standing up against the R & U shack, wishing away like anything that Steph would come out and give the signal. Only I surely wished she'd hurry 'cause it was getting wetter and colder by the minute. I leaned away from the shack for a moment and tried to see if the third-floor lights of Headquarters were still on. They were. I wondered if Selly was still up there. No, Selly would be in the club. He was always in the club on nickel beer nights. I was always in the club on nickel beer nights. OK, I'd give her just fifteen more minutes then in I'd go. Yessir, just fifteen more minutes and into the club I'd go. Maybe she was in there ripping off a piece with Lou? No, Lou was on duty, she couldn't be ripping off a piece with him. Well, where the hell was she then?

I leaned back against the shack and thought about all the good beer I was missing. Sure, that's what I thought about, all right.

•

I'd come to the unit about four or five months before, straight out of Fort Bragg, North Carolina. When the commander of my unit at Bragg found out I wasn't going to jockstrap for him he wanted me the hell out. I wasn't going to jump out of any airplanes for him, either. It was all right with me, being sent to Germany. Hell, I wouldn't have even been in the Army in the first place if I hadn't broken my leg at the Cleveland training camp up in Hiram. The Cleveland Browns! Pro football was a crappy way of making a living.

In Germany the Old Man tried to talk me into playing ball for the unit team, but by then I was through playing games.

"We gotta think of the unit's morale, Murray," he said to me.

"Sir," I replied, "we have to think of my leg too." Anyway, as things turned out they didn't turn out too badly. I became unofficial assistant coach of the unit team and didn't have to really do anything. It was just as well because I was finished jockstrapping for anyone then: the Browns, State, anyone.

After I went and busted my leg in the Brown training camp, and after I'd hung around Columbus until Smokey told me to get the hell out, I volunteered for the draft. It was as easy as that. If I'd known how easy it would be, I would have volunteered after high school, or during my freshman year at State, but—well, you know—I just never got around to it then. My old man wanted me to sue the Browns, and Elsie Whitemore's father up in Shaker Heights wanted me to join his real estate business. But I wasn't ready for any of that jazz just then. I was ready for the US Army.

My old man didn't have anything to say about it this time, either.

I took my basic at Dix for eight weeks, and they kept me on for about three or four months more teaching me all about the code and radios. Then they farmed me out to Fort Bragg where I never even used a radio or the code. Someone saw my Form 20 and remembered that I had made second team

Big Ten and right away, bingo, I was made a special services clerk until the C. O. there found out I wasn't going to play ball or jump out of airplanes. Why does everyone want you to play ball just because you may have played ball once? At State I bet only four or five people in the entire school knew I had majored in math, not phys ed. I wasn't exactly what you would call a ball of fire in math, but at least no one could accuse me of taking any gut basket-weaving courses. And when I graduated at least I could say I had learned something. I learned how goddam hard differential equations were, that's what I learned. I also learned how to pull out to my right and lead the power sweep. I never made the dean's list, but I did make second team Big Ten as an offensive guard and I didn't flunk anything except "Great Books" and that was only because I refused to finish *The Brothers Karamazov*.

After Bragg, I waited around at Dix for a while, then was shipped over to that repple-depple in Frankfurt. While they considered my Form 20 and security clearance I didn't do much of anything, but then, just as I was acquiring a taste for Dortmunder Union Bier, they pipelined me the hell out of Frankfurt to the boondocks of West Germany, to an old Army town called Faulenberg.

At first, because of my personality and good looks, I was temporarily assigned as unit librarian, but eventually I ended up as R & U clerk. This was mainly due to the fact that the R & U shack was situated down by the football field and care of the field would be my most important duty. At least until Frankfurt OK'd my clearance. When I told the Old Man that jockstrapping was definitely out of the question, he threatened to send me up to Operations where I belonged. "Murray," he'd shout. "You play ball for me and I'll play ball for you."

But I'd just smile and point to my leg and mention the fact that I had a Class C physical profile and it might look funny to the IG if I reinjured my leg playing football when I wasn't even fit for front line duty.

The Old Man'd mutter and fuss about this and talk about making me a security guard, or sending me up the hill to Operations, but he just never seemed to realize that I *wanted* to go up the hill to Operations.

If they'd have sent me up to Operations the whole business with Steph would never have started. But they didn't send me up to Operations, they kept me on as R & U clerk and assistant football coach. And I went ahead and met Stephanie Plummer.

It was innocent enough, all right, but stupid. That sort of thing was always stupid, wasn't it? Chuck would have thought it was stupid. Anyway, I first met her when I was temporary unit librarian. She came in to return some overdue books one day and we talked a bit because I was new to the unit then; and it being a real friendly and hospitable unit, why naturally my platoon leader's wife thought it only her duty to be cordial to all the new men. I guess I was also considered some sort of nut because I was the only one to refuse to play ball for the Old Man, and word of my refusal must have made the rounds rather quickly.

The only other time anyone came close to arguing with the Old Man was when Lou Plummer refused to go along with a bunch of crap during the Sandwich Report Affair. Lou was right, of course, but he ended up with all the shit details—meaning he was assigned to be officer in charge of the motor pool, mess hall, and repair and utilities. He was popular with the troops, though, even if he was sort of funny-looking.

His wife, Stephanie, was something else again. She was real pretty, in a windswept, phony, Southern sort of way. Her drawl at times must have made even the residents of Greenville, South Carolina, shudder. They had a little two-year-old girl, but somehow they never really gave you the impression that they were parents, you know what I mean.

After a while I got to know Lou real well, especially since we spent a lot of time working in R & U together. One day he asked me down to his apartment in the Dependent Area for dinner and I accepted, figuring what the hell, it would sure beat eating in the mess hall again. So that day, after we'd finished repairing the goalposts, we drove around to Dependent Building 8905. Steph didn't know we were coming and we barged right in on her.

"We got some company, sugah," Lou called out as we went into the apartment.

Stephanie stuck her fuzzy red head out of the kitchen and said, "What?" Then she saw me and got all flustered and excited. "Lawse, sugah," she screamed. "You could have at least given me a little warnin'."

"That's all right," Lou answered, pouring me a healthy shot of bourbon and then pulling a bottle of Beck's Bier out of the refrigerator to go with it. "It's only Murray. No one under the rank of PFC counts, right?"

I laughed 'cause I didn't know what else to do, then Lou showed me his little girl, Pat, and we went into the living room and played with her, and drank, and waited around until chow was served.

Steph was apologetic about the dinner, which was something close to a macaroni and cheese casserole. "Bet you were going to have something good up at the mess hall, weren't you, Murray?" she said.

"Huh uh," I mumbled.

"They had," Lou replied. "Salisbury steak, green beans, mashed potatoes and 'Answer' Cake."

"I'm real sorry," Steph said.

"It's all right," I stated cheerfully. "It's only hamburger."

"That's the wrong attitude, private," Lou said. Then he

turned to Steph. "I thought we were going to have a roast or something, sugah? I thought you were going to the commissary today?"

"Ah ran out of money."

"What happened to that ten dollars scrip I gave you last night?"

"Ah had a 'do," Steph said, smiling at me. "Like it?"

"A what?" Lou asked.

"A 'do, sugah." She touched her hair. "A *hair*-do."

"Sheeessss," Lou sighed. "Murray," he whispered to me, "Don't get married."

"Now you just hush, sugah."

"Don't get married to someone who doesn't even like to cook."

Steph stood up and started to clear the table. "Now you have nothing to complain about, Harold Lou. You knew all about that before you asked me to marry you."

Lou laughed and leaned back in his chair. "Ah surely do wish we could have a roast, though, sugah. I surely do wish we could."

And then it sort of started. Lou asked me to babysit for them every so often and, of course, every time I went down to babysit I saw Steph, and although she and Lou always seemed to be fussing about something, I got along real well with her. Pretty soon I was spending less and less time at the club drinking beer and more and more time down at the Plummer apartment, drinking bourbon, talking with Steph, and babysitting.

That isn't all I did, of course. I mean I did have my R & U duties, and we did play a little at being in the Army, but I also managed to get over to Paris on a couple of weekend passes with Selly and Wilse. Those were great times. We used to hang out around American Express on Rue Scribe and pick up American college girls just waiting to be picked up by people who knew what the real Paris was all about. Good times were had by just about all.

But sooner or later the shit was bound to hit the fan, and hit the fan it did. One night when I was in the Plummer kitchen getting some ice, Steph came barging in and pointed out the window up toward Headquarters. "Which one is your room?" she asked.

I stood next to her and looked across the football field, the perimeter fence, the Dependent Building playground. "That one, on the corner," I said, pointing it out.

"That's the one I thought it was," she said gaily, charging back out of the kitchen.

From that time on whenever I hit the sack at night, and whenever I got up in the morning, I'd stare out that corner window and try to figure out what was going on behind the third window from the left on the second floor of Dependent Building 8905. It got so bad that Selly, who had the sack next to mine, used to kid me about it. I think somewhere along the line Selly knew what was going on, but he never tried to bug me. "You know what you're doing, Pete?" he'd ask me sometimes. And then, when I'd say I knew what I was doing, he'd change the subject.

Selly came from up in Michigan and absolutely hated the Bucks and just about everything they stood for. We argued about this fact a good deal of the time at the club, but to tell the truth I wasn't so sure I was in favor of what the Bucks stood for myself a good deal of the time. I will say this—that Michigan game my senior year was absolutely the toughest game I've ever been in. We really knocked some heads together in that game. Even though we managed to win, 21–7, it was still a close, bitter battle. Hell, that game wasn't a battle, it was a war.

Then, one Saturday evening late in September, it really did hit the fan. All the officers had this big Happy Hour party celebrating something or other, and so naturally Lou asked me if I wanted the duty that evening. I saw no reason to decline—I mean it would sure beat just hanging around the barracks, right?

So after I was nicely settled, the kid asleep, and a glass of bourbon in my hand, the phone rang. Lou usually called up sometime during the evenings I babysat to see if everything was all right, so naturally I thought it was him and answered in my usual semimilitary fashion.

"Lieutenant Plummer's apartment, Babysitter Murray speaking, sir."

"Murray?" a soft little Southern voice asked. "Murray, is that you? This is Stephanie."

I could tell it was Stephanie. "Hi," I replied, not knowing what else to say.

"Murray, are you sober?"

I wasn't the least bit sober, but I said I was.

"Murray," she whispered. "Tell me the truth, do you have a little girlfriend back home?"

I shook my head, then answered no.

"Are you madly in love with some little dolly?"

I shook my head again.

"*Are* you?"

"Huh uh," I answered.

Steph was silent for a few moments.

"Hello?" I asked.

She answered quickly, little-girllike and frightened. "Oh Pete," she whispered. "I'm in love with you."

For once in my life I was speechless. I mean usually I can think of something to say no matter what has happened. I sure know what I should have said. I should have said, "Get serious," or that I did have a girl back home after all, or something—anything. But I didn't. I didn't say one cotton-picking word. All I did was laugh.

"Oh, lawse," Steph whined. "Oh, lawse, please don't laugh at me, Murray."

"I'm not laughing at you, honest."

"Y'are," she answered, sounding for all the world like she was about to cry.

"No, I'm not . . . really . . ." I started to go on, but I was stopped by a click on the other end of the line. The rest of the evening I just sat there, right by the phone, waiting for it to ring again, but it never did. When Steph and Lou finally staggered in I was asleep on the couch. Steph didn't even look at me, she just moved right smartly into the latrine.

"She had too much," Lou whispered to me.

So had I.

And that's when it really started. I was glued to that corner window from then on, and after a while, I could make out Steph looking back at me, too. And then . . .

And then there was that cold, wet perimeter fence again. I walked up next to it and put my hand on its clammy wire. I heard some stray shouts coming from the club and then I heard tattoo blow over the loudspeaker. God, it was miserable out there. "Come on out, Steph," I whispered. "Please come on out."

How many times had we tried to break it off? Twenty, a hundred, I don't know. There was only one thing that was going to break it off—my leave. Either my leave or three thousand miles. Three thousand miles would have been easier, but I wasn't about to be shipped back home until my tour was up. So the leave would have to do the trick. Munich, Paris, Italy, Switzerland, I don't know, just any place except western West Germany. We had been planning at one time to meet in Munich, but things were bad enough, and it was time for things to stop.

Back at State I'd been going hot and heavy with Elsie Whitemore my senior year, but I broke up with her just before we went out to the Rose Bowl. She'd wanted to come out to LA to see the game, but I told her I wouldn't have any time for her and that if she came I'd ask for my pin back. I asked for my pin back a little later anyway, but that's besides the point. The thing is, sometimes you just had to break things off. And bugging out someplace is sometimes the best way. And in just fifteen, no fourteen now, more hours I'd be off on leave.

But I still stood by that fence. God, I was lonely. God, I was cold. God, I wished that Chuck hadn't been killed in Korea.

And then I said the hell with it. I mean just what the hell was I doing, anyway? I was waiting in the rain for some twenty-two-year-old mother to flash her cigarette lighter, that's what I was doing. What a stupid-ass thing to be doing. What was wrong with me anyway? According to *Stars & Stripes* Hungarian kids my age were there in Budapest fighting the Russians. John Wayne would have been over there helping them. Maybe even Chuck. . . . What was the matter with me?

I hit my hand up against the side of the fence. So, I'd go off on leave without seeing her. What was so earth-shaking about that? "Raus," I shouted out loud. "Raus, you bastards!"

And then I turned my back to the fence and stomped off to the club. It was stupid to miss all of nickel beer night.

I gave Curt a quarter scrip and picked up five bottles of Beck's, then walked over to where Selly and Horse were sitting, a large bowl of popcorn between them. "How's the window tonight?" Horse asked.

Selly didn't give me a chance to answer. Good old Selly. "What's the magic number, Pete?"

I looked at my watch. "Fourteen," I said. "Where's Wilse?"

"Writing letters."

Wilse was always writing letters. Personally, I'd just about given up that sort of thing. I wrote home once in a while, but what was I going to write home about, playing around with some officer's wife? I did write a few letters to this crazy old math prof I had. He was a great old guy. I don't even think he knew I was on the football team. I mean, I don't think it would have made any difference to him one way or the other as long as I was interested in math. He always had this crazy idea that I was going to try for my Master's. He was a goofy old guy all right. At the end of his classes he used to be almost completely covered with chalk dust.

"What are you going to do when you get out, Pete?" Selly asked. Selly was always asking me things like that. I told him what I always told him, that I didn't know what I was going to do. I didn't, either. I had thought a little bit about getting my Master's, but I knew I was just kidding myself. My grades hadn't really been good enough.

"Why don't you give the Browns another chance?" Horse said. "They still interested?"

I nodded. But I was tired of hearing about the Browns and how I had almost made it with them. You want to know the truth? I didn't even come close to making it with them and not because I busted my leg either. I didn't come close to making it with them 'cause I was loafing, that's why. And if you loaf, if you really don't care, you might as well hang up the jock before you start because sooner or later you're going to get clobbered. I got clobbered, I know.

I guess I did want to play pro ball again, though, but mostly because I didn't know what else to do.

"Maybe I'll re-up," I said, taking a handful of popcorn. "Think of all them good benefits."

"Sheeet," Horse replied. "Who ever heard of a US re-upping?"

"Tommy Fillmore re-upped."

"Him," Horse scoffed. "He was an NG. He *liked* the Army."

"Three square meals a day."

"Take all you want, but eat all you take."

Then Selly started talking about politics. He had been trying to arouse some interest in the election, but no one was really as shook up about it as Selly was. I mean, we all knew who was going to win, so what was the use? I never particularly liked talking about politics anyway. Especially over there in Deutschland. That's just about all they had in *Stars & Stripes* though, election news, sports, and comics. I often wondered what the rest of the world was supposed to do while we figured out our politics—stop and take a pee? Everyone except Selly knew who was going to win anyway. Why is it that the smartest guys sometimes know the least?

Then Selly talked about the Hungarian thing. "What do you think they're gonna do?" he asked.

"Who?"

"The Hungarians. They kicked the Russians out of Budapest, what's gonna happen now?"

Horse shrugged and opened a new bottle of Beck's. "Who cares? Them Russian troops decide to come back, they'll come back, that's all. It's none of our business."

"It *is* our business," Selly answered, getting a little excited. "Pappy McDonald's been talking to one of those guys in Budapest on the MARS net. They think we're coming to help them."

"Yeah, that's all we need," Horse said. "To play games with the Russians. They'd never call out the troops."

"Especially in an election year," I said.

Selly looked at me. "You think that might be it? Jesus, that'd be terrible, terrible."

"What those people really need," Horse said, "is John Wayne."

Yeah, I thought, that's just what they need.

Murphy Bates and Wilse then came over to our table with some more beer, and immediately the conversation turned to Old War Stories, but since I had already heard these very same Old War Stories many times, my thoughts turned elsewhere. Besides, none of us had even been in a war.

My thoughts turned to Dependent Building 8905 and the inhabitants thereof.

At first, all Steph and I had a chance to do was to meet when I came down to babysit and to look at each other through our respective windows.

Once, however, when I was babysitting Steph came back early, looking for her earrings supposedly, and we advanced the matter somewhat. I mean we at least got around to kissing each other. If that wasn't advancement, I don't know what was. Then we started meeting down by the fence at night and that worked out all right, when she could come out, 'cause we could talk and laugh and pass notes to each other and kiss through the fence. But when she couldn't come out it was pretty terrible. Especially when I had to watch their lights go off at night. I knew Steph and Lou were still sleeping with each other—I knew this 'cause I had asked—and far be it for me to deny anyone their own particular brand of marital pleasure, but it was still pretty miserable to be out there, waiting, when they hit the sack.

Of course, everyone knows I didn't have to be out there waiting, but that would have been the smart thing to do. Needless to say, I was more than a little confused in this momentous period of my life, and my advice to all youngsters who one day hope to play professional football for the Cleveland Browns is to avoid having affairs with married women, because affairs with married women tear your heart apart and everyone knows you can't play the pro game with a broken heart.

Once I asked Steph how she and Lou got along, you know, physically. "We get along terrible in bed," Steph said sadly. "Ah juss feel like an old dishrag." I didn't believe her, of course, but it made me feel pretty good at the time anyway. "Some of our biggest fusses," Steph continued, "are because Lou says I didn't respond properly."

Well, that was fine and goddam dandy, but it still wasn't much fun being out there by that fence and then seeing their lights go off at night. It sometimes liked to break me near in two.

All this was, of course, leading up to one thing: Doing It with her. I mean where else could a thing like this lead to? I only had about six or eight thousand good reservations, but they certainly weren't going to stand in my way. The trouble was, though, we didn't really have an opportunity. That is, we didn't have it for a while, not until Steph had to go over to the dental clinic in Kusel. Lou was OD at the time and asked me if I'd mind driving over to Kusel in their VW to pick her up. I didn't mind at all. On the way back from the clinic we parked for a while, but the weather did not smile upon us.

"Ah surely do wish it wasn't raining," she giggled. I did, too.

We started to hug and kiss anyway in record time. "I wish this were a big American car," I said.

"Why?" she giggled.

"You know."

"Huh uh. All you men ever think about is Nashes."

"I didn't even mention a Nash."

"You were thinking about one, weren't you, sugah . . . ?"

Well.

Suddenly there was a flash of light in the rear window. Steph jumped away from me quickly. "Gawd," she whispered.

I looked back and saw that it was only a car using the place where we were parked to turn around in.

"Was it the MPs?" she asked.

"Huh uh."

She shook her head. "This is terrible," she muttered. "Juss terrible. Ah think we better go."

But I didn't let her go. Soon we were all wrapped around each other again and it got very warm very quickly in that little old car.

"Steph?"

"Mmmmmmmmmmm?"

My hand found its way underneath her coat. "Steph?"

She opened her eyes. "Yes?"

"Let's go outside."

She looked at me for just a second, then nodded.

We both jumped out of the car quickly. It was a mistake, however. A wet, cold mistake. The rain was really coming down, but we had our minds made up. Oh yes, when your minds are made up you can do anything. Steph found a tree with a dry spot underneath. She spread her coat out, then whispered: "Love me, Pete. Oh, love me."

I put my arms around her and tried to love her. It wasn't warm and cozy anymore, though. In fact it was pretty terrible. But I'll say this, fans, I tried—I really did. But it was cold and raining and we both had all sorts of clothes on. I mean, basically, I'm a traditional son of a bitch and I wanted Our First Time at Doing It to be on a bed, see, with no clothes on, see, and with absolutely no rain coming down. But the truth was, it was raining, we did have clothes on, and the ground was wet, bumpy and hard.

And so it was no go. I mean the whole thing is pretty goddam ridiculous when I think about it now. It was ridiculous when I thought about it then, too.

"I'm sorry," she said when we were back in the car.

"It's my fault," I said.

She shook her head, then lit a cigarette. "It's not your fault. Do you want to go to the apartment?"

"No," I answered quickly. "Not in his bed."

"It's my bed, too."

"It's the taxpayers' bed," I stated, ending the discussion.

•

Along about this time I had the feeling that maybe I'd better put in for a transfer to someplace like Alaska. But I knew I would never be transferred again. Then I got the idea of going in to the Old Man and confessing everything. "Sir," I'd say. "I'm sort of in love with Lieutenant Plummer's wife and I think you'd better ship me back to the States, preferably not Fort Bragg, in the national interest."

And whenever I had this particular fantasy, the Old Man would look me squarely in the eye and say, "Murray, I appreciate your honesty, we're making you corporal and shipping you back tomorrow."

Of course, I knew it wouldn't happen like that. I knew the colonel would call Lou in, and then it would really hit the fan. I mean, I liked Lou, and I don't think he knew anything about it. So, what did I do? Nothing, that's what I did. I did put in for a ten-day leave, though, and that's just what I was getting—a ten-day leave. In just fourteen more hours.

After the Kusel fiasco we once decided to meet up in Heidelberg on a Saturday afternoon. But the night before, down at the fence, she told me she couldn't go. I asked her why.

"I couldn't get a babysitter," she laughed.

I didn't think it was as funny as she did.

"Tomorrow is the day of the Curse," she admitted.

"The what?"

"You know."

"Really? Tomorrow?"

She nodded. "Ever since I had Pat they don't come smack on schedule at all."

I looked at her closely. "I could tell," I said.

"You could? How could you tell?"

"I just could."

She got a little cross. "No you couldn't. Could you? Please tell me, how could you tell?"

"You have a big X right there on your forehead," I said.
She didn't think that was so funny after all.

"Hey, Pete."
"Hey, US."
"Pete."
I looked over at Horse and Selly, then shook my head.
"Where you been, fella?"
"Back home," I lied. "Thinking of all them Buckeyes."
"Yeah, sure," Selly said. "Home of Smokey Brandt."
"Where you going on your leave?"
"Everywhere," I replied, sweeping my hand onto another beer.
Lieutenant Plummer, OD helmet and all, walked into the club and came over to our table. The conversation stopped.
"How's it going, troops?" he asked.
"Fine, sir."
"Beer holding out all right?"
"Sure is, sir."
I could feel him looking at me, so I looked up. "When do you leave, Murray?"
"Noon."
"Going over to help those Hungarians?"
"Who knows?" I said.
"A big football player like you should be over there," Lou said, smiling craftily at me. "The Old Man would give his approval, I'm sure."
Sure, sure, sure, sure. Fortunately, Lou didn't really want to talk and started over to another table. Selly went back to talking about the election. I went toward the latrine. Halfway there I changed my mind and left the club, walking over to Headquarters through the cold mist. I walked up to room 29. The lights were still on so I checked over my AWOL bag, then took a good hot shower. Taps was blowing when I came back into the room, so I switched off the lights and climbed

into my sack. I turned on Selly's radio and listened to the AFN news for a while. Mostly election news, then one brief announcement about Hungary. I switched the radio off and looked up at the dark ceiling. And then I decided I better open the window. I needed that old fresh air, I decided. Yessir, that's why I went to that window all right.

I saw the signal as soon as I got there. At first I didn't believe it. But there it was again, twice, just like always. Oh crap. Oh crap almighty.

And before I could even think about signaling back, I was in my clothes and running down out of Headquarters, down behind the R & U shack.

Steph hadn't forgotten after all. She hadn't forgotten!

2

I could just make out her silhouette against the bank of mist. I ran up to the fence where it came closest to the R & U shack. "Hi," I whispered. I could hear her footsteps padding in my direction, and then there she was, right in front of me.

"Hi," she whispered in an out-of-breath voice, putting her hands on top of mine between the wires of the fence. "Hi."

We smiled at each other, then I leaned up against the fence and tried to get as close to her as I could. She bent her head next to the wires and we managed a small, wet, warm, stupid kiss.

"Hello," I said quietly. Her finger ran along the side of my thumb. Then she shivered just a bit.

"Lawse, I thought you'd never come," she complained. "Ah almost had to go back in."

"Come on," I said. "I've been out here almost all night."

"No, you haven't."

"Yes, I have. I was out here for almost two hours."

She looked down at the ground for a few seconds. "I'm sorry," she whispered. Then she looked right at me. "Were you really out here for two hours?"

I nodded. "I came out about eight thirty, then went to the club after tattoo. I was just getting into the sack when I saw the signal."

"I'm sorry," she said again. "I told you I didn't think I could make it."

"I know."

"I mean, Lou's OD again and the baby was waking up. Ah honestly thought that child would never go to sleep."

"It's all right."

She shook her head. "It's not all right. No, it's *not* all right. You were out here in the rain for almost two hours. You must really hate me."

"Come on," I said. "I don't hate you."

"Ah know," she replied in a small voice. "Ah have to go in right away."

"You do?"

"The baby might wake up again. Lou might call. Oh, Pete, I'm beginning to feel guilty every time I come out here. And then I feel guilty when I don't come out. . . . I don't know."

Her hand fell away from mine and I clutched onto the fence tightly. "I'm sorry," I said.

Steph looked right at me. "Pete, I never want there to be a misunderstand between us."

"There won't be, I promise." Her hands came back to the fence and rested on mine again.

"Lawse," she whispered. "How ah do love you."

"I love you, too."

"How much?"

I started to say, what? But then I saw her smiling, sad eyes, twinkling just a bit. "Well, how much do you think you're worth, you middle-aged Southern woman, you?"

"I'm not middle-aged."

I played with the belt of her trench coat. "All married women are middle-aged. What do you have on underneath?"

"Wouldn't you like to know?"

"Mmmm-hmmmmmm."

"My PJs."

"The short ones or the long ones?"

"Wouldn't you like to know? Besides, what difference does it make?"

"The short ones or the long ones?" I asked again.

"Ah don't think it's any of your business, young soldier."

"Why do you have the short ones on?"

"Why not?"

"Your legs are going to catch cold."

"They already are cold—that's why I have to go in right away."

"'Bye."

She flashed a quick look at me, then started to turn. Just as quickly, she jumped back to the fence. "Why do you care what kind of PJs I have on?"

"I don't know."

"Why?"

I looked up at the drizzling mist. "'Cause you told me once that you slept with the long ones on so that you could keep warm at night."

"So?" She smiled warmly at me.

"So, why don't you have the long ones on?"

She rubbed my fingers again and leaned her face up close to mine. "'Cause Lou's OD, that's why."

I looked at her for a few moments. "What were we talking about?"

"What? Just now? You were being silly."

"No, before I was being silly. . . . Never mind. Can you meet me tomorrow?"

"Tomorrow?"

"I mean Saturday."

She shook her head. "I can't."

"Why not?" I asked a second or two later. "It was your idea."

"I have to take the baby to the doctor."

"I thought you were going to do that next week?"

She shook her head. "It has to be Saturday."

"Can't you really meet me?"

"Huh uh."

"This may be our last chance."

She looked at me very closely. "It may be." She started to say something else, but stopped.

"What?"

"Nothing."

"What?"

"Pete, I'm sorry, but I don't think I can take any more chances."

"Just . . . ?" I looked over at her, but she was staring down at the wet ground.

"Pete?"

"Yeah?"

"Are you mad?"

"Huh uh," I answered truthfully. "Am I acting silly?"

"No," she said. "You're not acting silly." She leaned up to the fence and we kissed lightly. "I'm sorry," she whispered when we were through.

"What for?"

"For everything."

"If you can't, you can't, that's all."

She smiled at me. "What would we do, if I could come that is?"

I caressed the tips of her fingers for a few seconds. "Well," I stated seriously. "Maybe I'd meet you at the Hofbrauhaus, see, and then show you the sights of Old München."

"Come on, what would we really do?"

"You know what we'd do."

"Tell me."

I whispered very softly. "We'd find us a hotel room, and once we found that room we'd make love from the minute we stepped inside until the minute we left."

Steph leaned forward for another kiss. If anyone had been watching they would have thought we were completely out of our minds. "That sounds so lovely," she whispered.

I was going to go on, to explain in a little greater detail what we'd be doing, but I could see her shivering away like anything in that soggy trench coat of hers and knew she must have been freezing her can off. "I'm sorry," I said.

"*Don't* be sorry," she answered quickly. "Don't ever be

sorry. It all sounds so wonderful. . . . If I did manage to come you wouldn't give me instructions, would you?"

"Instructions? What for?"

"You know: Doing It?"

"Why should I give you instructions?" I stared at her for a few moments. "Come up to Munich, Steph."

She giggled, then shook her head two or three times. "Oh, I sure wish I could. You have no idea how I wish I could, but Lou's getting suspicious and I'm sure I've been talking in my sleep."

"God, what do you say?"

"I don't know, but I dream about you all the time. Wild dreams." She giggled for a moment, then frowned. "And that's why I can't meet you. I'm sure Lou's getting suspicious. Last week he started giving me big speeches about neglecting the baby and getting the housework done and buying meat for dinner."

"That doesn't mean he's suspicious."

"Yes, it does. I don't even get up to cook him his breakfast anymore."

"So? I like you the way you are."

"C'mon," she said.

"I do. I wouldn't want you to change one bit."

"Ah believe you do mean it . . . even if it is foolish."

"What's so foolish about it?"

" 'Cause you don't know how selfish and possessive ah am, that's why. You'd just grow tired of me and start giving me instructions."

"I wouldn't give you *any* instructions. Why do you keep saying that?"

" 'Cause that's what would happen."

I shook my head. "Everyone doesn't have to change just because they get married."

"Yes they do. Because when you get married you have responsibility. And you spell that with a capital R."

"Everyone has responsibility."

"Not like when you're married, though. Not like when you have children and are absolutely dependent upon your husband for food, clothing and shelter. If Lou left me what would I do? I don't really know how to do anything."

"Lou wouldn't leave you . . ."

"He would if he found out."

"Well . . . maybe everything'll work out all right."

"How?"

"What do you mean?"

"Just how is everything going to work out all right? Ah want to know."

I wasn't too cotton-picking happy about the way the conversation was going. But there wasn't much I was able to do about it either. "I don't know exactly, but if we want it to work out, it'll work out."

"But *how?*"

I hit the side of the fence. "I'll pass us a miracle."

"That's just what I mean, really. It's just all too impossible. I guess my middle-class morality is catching up with me all of a sudden."

"Your middle-class morality or your Southern morality?"

"What difference does it make? Once it's caught up, it's caught up."

"God!" I said, hitting the fence again. "I'm coming over there."

"Why?"

" 'Cause I want to finish this talk with my arms around you, that's why."

"OK."

"You *want* me to come over?"

"Sure."

I started to climb the wet fence.

"Pete?" she called softly.

"Yeah?"
"Ah really do have to go in in a second."
I stopped climbing and looked at her. "Do you want me to come over there?"
"I don't know," she said suddenly. "I just don't know."
I slid back down the fence. "You don't know?" I asked. She nodded her head, then shook it quickly, then looked down at the ground. I hit the fence with my hand again. "Why does this fence have to be here?" I shouted.
"Shhhhhhhhh."
"Why does there have to be a fence?"
She looked right at me and spoke quietly. "There always will be a fence."
I had a definite sinking feeling that she just might possibly be right. I mean I couldn't really blame her for not wanting to take any more chances. She'd taken so many chances as it was; half the time, I guess, I didn't even begin to realize what sort of chances she was taking. I had several good escape clauses: I was leaving on furlough in a few hours, then going home in six or seven months. She was probably going to spend the rest of her natural, Southern, cotton-picking way of life with Lou. I wonder if a quick roll in the hay would have solved any of our problems? I mean, really solved them?
So, I wasn't feeling too red-hot out there by that miserable perimeter fence. The cold rain was still drizzling down and I was lonely, even though Steph was only about two or three feet away from me. I seriously considered giving up good Kraut beer because good Kraut beer always made me feel sentimental or horny or both. And it did me no real good to feel sentimental or horny or both when that fence was between us. But there we were. And there was that fence.
"Pete?" she whispered. "Pete, I have to go in now."
"OK."

"Pete?"

I looked through the fence at her.

"Please don't hate me, Pete. Please don't hate me."

"I don't hate you," I said softly. "You know that."

She looked little-girllike again as she stared down at her funny, dirty sneakers. "You will."

"Why?"

" 'Cause." She kicked at the bottom of the fence with one foot.

"Why, Steph?"

" 'Cause . . ." She stopped. "You're absolutely going to hate me."

"God, tell me why."

I tried to reach my fingers through the fence so I could touch and reassure her, but she moved away. Then she took a real deep breath. "Pete, this isn't easy for me to tell you, but I have to tell you. I have to. I love you very much, I really do and I want you to understand that. I love you more than I've ever loved anyone." She thought for a second or two, then went on. "But I don't hate Lou. I can't hate Lou. . . . And I know he loves me in his own way. It's just something that we're going to have to work out."

"I know that," I said when she paused. "We both know that."

She reached into her trench coat pocket and pulled out a Kleenex, then wiped her nose. When she was through she put her hands back into her pockets and looked right at me.

"Pete," she said. "I think I'm pregnant." She turned around and started to walk away from the fence.

"Come back," I yelled. "Steph!"

I could see her shake her head as she walked away. I put my hands up onto the fence and pulled myself up. I managed to get over the barrier with little trouble, but slipped in the mud when I jumped down. I scrambled to my feet, then slid over the damp, cold ground until I caught up with her. I grabbed her from behind and wrapped my arms around her stomach.

"It's OK," I whispered. "Everything is OK."

She shook her head again and started to cry. "No, it's not. It's not all right."

I just held her for a while, not saying anything, not knowing what to say anyway.

"I'm sorry," she whimpered after a few minutes, leaning back against me. "I'm sorry."

"Don't be sorry. You're going to have a baby."

She turned and faced me. "But I don't want a baby. I don't want one."

"Then why . . . ?" I stopped and looked at the dark mist. "I wish it were mine," I whispered.

She put her arms around my waist. "So do I. Oh, so do I."

"Are you sure? About the baby?"

She played with the collar of my field jacket. "I'm sure," she said.

We were both silent for a while. Then I looked down at her. "When did it happen?"

"When did what happen?"

"You know."

She moved away just a little bit. "I don't know."

"You must know."

"Pete, what good would it do?"

"I'm just curious. When did it happen?"

"I'm not sure."

"What do you mean?"

"I mean I'm just not sure. Lou's been pretty active lately."

"Come on, Steph, you must know when."

"No," she said, moving still further away. "You want to punish yourself and I won't let you."

"I don't want to punish myself. I just want to know what I was doing at the time, that's all."

"Pete, don't."

"I just want to know if I was waiting out here, or watching through the window, or what."

"Pete, *please!*"

"It's all right, I don't blame you."

She bit her lip for a moment. "You're the most wonderful person I've ever met, Pete. You really are."

I looked up into the wet air. "We're going to be a little sentimental, folks."

She grabbed my arms. "Please stop. Please! I have to go in."

"OK, go in."

"I don't want to leave you like this."

"How do you want to leave me?"

She thought for a moment. "I don't want you to be unhappy."

I blew some air through my nose and stared at her. "I think maybe I'll go join the Foreign Legion or something. The only trouble is, I hate deserts. I wonder what you do if you're in the Foreign Legion and hate deserts?"

"Please, please, *please!*"

"Well, what do you want me to say? OK, I'm happy. I knew it was never going to work out anyway."

Steph cried again and I was about to put my arms back around her when we both heard the noise. I turned and saw a flashlight shine up against the side of the R & U shack. I looked back at Steph, but she was already running toward Dependent Building 8905 through the mist. I didn't shout out goodbye.

In fact I lay down on the wet, cold ground and held my breath. Then I saw the dull glare of the flashlight again through the mist. Like Br'er Rabbit—or was it Br'er Fox?—I just lay low.

And then I thought I heard a voice call out cautiously: "Murray? Murray, y'down here?"

I didn't answer. I lay just as I was for about twenty minutes, feeling as wet and cold and miserable as I'd never felt before. Then I crept to my feet and walked back to the fence. It was twice as difficult climbing back over. It shouldn't have been, but it was.

I didn't take the chance of having Lou find me, so I snuck down behind the PX and went over to the MARS shack behind the 3rd Platoon barracks. There was a light on in the window so I went in.

Sergeant Benson and Pappy were alone in the shack, listening to the big radio.

"Murray!" Pappy exclaimed, looking up briefly. "You is the last person I thought I'd ever see in here."

"Where else is there to go on a night like this?"

"Nickel beer night, too," Pappy said, fiddling with the dial. "What can we do you for, Murray? A phone-patch home?"

"Huh uh."

Benny coughed and looked down at my muddy trousers and torn field jacket. "I like your uniform, Murray."

"Yeah," Pappy responded, not even bothering to look. After a few more fiddles with the dial he turned to me. "You don't speak Hungarian, do you?"

"I don't even speak good Deutsch."

"Balls," Sergeant Benson said. "I thought all you US college boys spoke five or six languages."

I looked down at Pappy. "Did you speak to one of those Hungarians?"

"How the hell can he speak to him if he can't speak the language?"

In the middle of a burst of static we all heard a faint voice. After about thirty seconds of garbled reception the voice faded out. Pappy fiddled furiously with the dials, but there were only occasional scratches of static.

"Balls," he swore, beating his hand against the side of the set. "We should be helping them poor bastards. We should be doing something."

I was going to ask what could we do, but decided not to. I looked around the shack for a few moments, then walked quietly out the door. No one said goodbye.

When I got back up to the room, Selly whispered over to me that Lou had been making the rounds.

"I know," I said, getting into the sack.

"You know what you're doing, Pete?" he asked a little later.

Good old Selly. "Sure," I answered. "I know what I'm doing."

What a liar I was.

At least I didn't look out that window. I knew what was outside of that cotton-picking window. The mist. The mist and that miserable fence.

And there was no more need to look at that.

3

We had some pretty good plays at State, even if we never passed very much, but the one I liked best was a counter play where I trapped the defensive right guard. Actually, it was only a simple reverse, but after a whole game of plowing ahead for three or four yards (and a cloud of dust) it really shook up the opposition. Hoppy scored against Iowa, and we opened up the Indiana game with the counter play. The Wolverines stopped it cold, but we whipped the Wolverines by just plain popping leather. The play worked well in the Rose Bowl, too, before a nationwide TV audience.

I was thinking about this particular play up there in Munich. I was in the world-renowned Hofbrauhaus, sort of semi-waiting around until Saturday for Steph. I knew she wasn't going to come, but I had to give her every last chance, right? Anyway, Steph and I were through. It was one thing to have an affair with a married woman, but something else again to have an affair with a pregnant married woman. I mean one person can only be so stupid. It's not easy to know that the person you think you might be in love with is pregnant by her own husband.

Besides thinking about that good counter play, I also thought about what might have happened if I had gone into the Army after high school. There was a good chance I might not have even been sent to Korea. But then, who knows, maybe I would have—maybe I would have been killed just like Chuck. Maybe my old man had been right.

But I didn't go into the Army. And Chuck was killed. And I did break my leg. And Steph was pregnant. I mean, what can you do once something is over? Nothing, that's what you can do.

I read *Stars & Stripes* on the train going up to Munich, but the news was just about the election, or Hungary, or Egypt, or college football. Even Steve Canyon was dull. When I'd signed out for leave, Lou was in the orderly room and called me into his office. I thought he might be calling me in for something else, but it turned out to be about this Hungarian thing. He really thought that I should go over there, to try and help. I asked him what he thought I could do, and he leaned back in his chair and thought for a moment or two before answering. "Well," he said after a while, "there may not be anything you can actually do, but at least you'd be there and see what really goes on."

"Maybe they'll call us all out," I said.

Lou shook his head. "Not a chance. They'll never call us out a few days before an election. The UN'll get around to talking about it, but that's about all they'll do."

"Do you think they should call us out?"

He smiled. "Who knows?" He stood up and put out his hand. "Have a good leave, Pete."

If he was suspicious about anything he sure didn't show it. We shook hands, and then I left for the Bahnhof. As expected, the train to Munich left right on time. And then there I was in the Hofbrauhaus.

And I sat there, all Friday evening, thinking about how fouled up I was and wishing that I was back in Columbus getting ready for Northwestern instead of just sitting there staring at those overweight steins of good Kraut beer.

I couldn't help but overhear the conversation this guy was having with a chick at the table right next to mine. I listened to them a while without looking up. Then I looked up at them without listening. She had long, blonde hair, an old camel-hair coat thrown around her shoulders, and was wearing a pair of filthy tennis shoes on her feet. It was the tennis shoes that did it, I think. Steph had always worn filthy tennis shoes.

They were arguing this way and that about Hungary. The guy was either queer or British or both. I mean just because some British guys sound queer doesn't exactly mean they really are. Heck, some of the biggest tigers I've ever known were British. Anyway, I listened to them talk about this revolt, or whatever it was, and they sure seemed to be furious with Americans in general, and the American Way of Life in particular. They were equally bitter about the Voice of America, and other aspects of Creeping McCarthyism, as they called it. After a while, and after a few more good beers, I joined their interesting conversation.

"So, what do you expect us to do?" I asked.

They both looked over at me for a second, then looked back at each other and continued their own conversation, this time a little more quietly.

So I said the hell with it and went into the latrine and pee-ed up against the wall. God, I hated those Kraut johns where you had to pee up against the wall. I really did. Anyway, I was peeing up against this wall, when the guy—that British guy—came in and stood next to me. Naturally, I started up a conversation with him. I mean we were both peeing—right?—and we both spoke the same language.

"So what's really happening over there in Hungary?" I asked, real neighborly like.

He stared at me for a second, then looked back at the wall and said matter-of-factly, "The Russians have returned and are surrounding Budapest."

"No shit," I stated pleasantly. "And what are the British doing to stop them?"

He turned and looked at me again, then buttoned up his fly. He started to leave, then turned to me when he was in the doorway. I don't know why, but it takes me longer to pee than everyone else in the human race, especially when I have to pee up against a wall.

"We're trying to save the Suez Canal," he whined. Yes, it very definitely could be considered a whine. "We," continued my peeing buddy, "are at least doing *something.*" Then, and only then, he left.

When I finally got out of that latrine the guy and the girl were gone. I looked all over for them, but they very definitely had gone. And I very definitely had the blue spots. I only managed to see the blue spots every once in a very great while. Yes, I very definitely saw the once-in-a-great-while blue spots.

So I went back to my hotel. I mean, what else was I going to do when I had an attack of the blue spots?

Needless to say I had sort of a hangover the next morning. I don't usually get hangovers after drinking beer, but after drinking good Kraut beer I sometimes did. That same fat SFC back at the repple-depple in Frankfurt gave us a lecture about Kraut beer. "Young gentlemuns," he bellowed to us. "Whenever each and every one of you drinks good Kraut beer remember this one fact—that Kraut beer is three times as powerful as Stateside brew. So, when you are out having your young selves a ball at the US taxpayer's expense, remember to multiply the number of beers you have drunk by three to know where you stand, only I wouldn't stand too quickly. . . ." Big laugh.

I tried to do some push-ups, but push-ups never really helped me with hangovers, so I went to the latrine, shaved, dressed, drank some coffee and then went out into the cool, clear morning of November 3, 1956. I walked around for a while, then strolled over to the Isar and got to thinking about how I used to walk along the Olentangy on Saturday mornings before home games. Somehow it used to help calm pregame jitters walking along a slow-moving, dull-colored river. And it helped calm my hangover some, too. Then I started to think some more about where I was going to go on my leave. I figured that I should probably go down into Italy where it was a little warmer. Whip on down to Venice, then play it by ear from there. Yeah, that's what I should do: Go on down to Venice, ride all them gondolas, and drink a little vino. Great.

I started to walk back to the Bahnhof so I could check on trains to Venice. There were a lot of people out shopping, or getting out of work, or something—I mean, the streets were really crowded—so it took me a long time to get back to the Bahnhof. When I was finally at the Bahnhofplatz it was almost twenty of twelve. Old Steph had once said she'd meet me at noon, in the station post office, and—what the heck—it wouldn't do me any harm to check, right?

And then, right before I was going to cross over to the Bahnhof, there was this girl, this girl from the night before at the Hofbrauhaus. She was standing right there on the corner, holding out a donation can to the passersby. On one of her camel-haired arms was a band urging aid for the Hungarians. I pulled out a mark coin, walked over to her and slipped it smilingly into her can. She smiled back automatically, then her automatic smile turned into a quizzical frown.

"Do I know you?" she asked.

"*Ja wohl,*" I replied. "We're old Hofbrauhaus buddies."

"Oh yes, I remember," she said looking away. "You were smashed."

"I wasn't so smashed. How's business?"

She shrugged and accepted some pfennig from a passerby. "*Vielen Dank,*" she said sarcastically. "Goddam cheap krauts." Then she looked back at me. "Nice seeing you again—'bye."

"OK, OK," I said, looking at the traffic light, waiting for it to change. "Are you saving the world?"

"Sure," she replied quickly. "Why not? At least I'm trying." She turned and tried to get some donations from a crowd of men marching swiftly down the sidewalk. "Goddam cheap krauts," she repeated.

"What's your name?" I asked.

"What's it to you?"

"*Macht nichts* to me."

"Lynn Walther," she answered without looking at me, but somehow not quite so hostilely.

"So," I said. "What brings you to Munich?"

"What's it look like? I'm working my way to Vienna, that's why I'm here in Munich."

I pointed to her donation can. "You mean . . . ?"

"Yeah, yeah, yeah," she said scowling. "The end justifies the means. How the fuck else can I get to Vienna? Everyone else went off without me." All of a sudden she looked at me with a reasonable amount of interest. "Are you going to Vienna?"

Venice, Vienna, who the hell cared? "Maybe," I replied. "What's in Vienna?"

"The goddam opera, what do you think? Look, let's talk about it, all right? Buy me some coffee?"

"OK," I said. "Let's have us some coffee."

So we went and had some coffee.

Twenty minutes later I decided that I should definitely go to Vienna. I mean, why not? The girl was trying to catch up with some of her friends, and when she caught up with them they were then all going to go to the Hungarian border to see what was up.

"There are all those poor people in Budapest," she said angrily, lighting up a Gauloise. "And what are we doing about it? What is the Great American Army doing about it?"

"Nothing," I said. "I'm in the Great American Army, you know."

She nodded at me, blowing some smoke into the air. "Jesus Christ, I know that. I can tell a GI at twenty paces, an American at a hundred."

"So what happened to your friend?"

"Who? Oh, last night?" She shrugged. "I don't know, he was pissed off on account of the sleeping arrangements or something. Why don't you take me to Vienna?"

"What would the sleeping arrangements be?"

She laughed. "Who knows? You're funny. I'm trying to catch up with my friends anyway."

"Did you break up with your friend, the guy from last night?"

"Break up? Hell, we were never really going together. There was nothing to break up. I'm not about to get involved with anyone, let me tell you. I'm what they call the uninvolved, sullen divorcee."

"You don't look so sullen to me. You don't look divorced, either."

"Let me tell you something, I don't feel divorced. Does that bug you? Sorry you bought me coffee?"

"Huh uh," I protested.

"Are *you* going with anyone?" I shook my head. "Look," she said earnestly. "Why don't we go to Vienna? No strings or involvements or anything. Just help me get a ticket, OK? We can play games for six hours on the train."

"Games?"

She hit me on the arm. "Word games, what do you think? Jesus, you're square, you know that?"

I knew that. A pig's eye I knew that. "OK," I decided. "I'll help you get to Vienna. No involvements or commitments or anything. I'm really on my way to Venice."

"Sure, sure, sure," she said. "Everyone goes to Venice by way of Vienna."

We promised to meet in the Bahnhof in an hour, so I whipped back to my hotel, collected my stuff, then paid the bill. Why not go to Vienna, I thought. I was free, single, and almost twenty-three years old. Why not do anything?

Just to make sure, though, I checked the station post office.

I peeked in, then froze. God, she was there, waiting for me! Oh Jesus, Steph, why didn't you stay at home? What did she want? I peeked again to make sure. It was Steph all right, looking out-of-place, and frightened, and very, very lonely.

Go home, Steph, I whispered. Go home. It's over with.

Then I walked slowly, and carefully, away. I went up to a ticket window and bought two second-class tickets to Vienna, and the appropriate schnellzug card. The train was due to leave at 1330 hours, and there I was—all hot to trot—standing up a pregnant married woman for a girl whose name I couldn't even remember.

Well, anyway, goodbye, Steph. Goodbye.

She was almost late. Not quite, but almost. She came charging through that Bahnhof a mile a minute, her camel-haired coat streaming along behind her. "Come on, stupid," she called to me. "Or we'll miss that fuckin' schnellzug."

We didn't miss it, though. We rode that train all the way to Linz, then changed to another train which took us to Vienna's Westbahnhof. She talked and talked: about how stupid all Americans were, how the Republican party was full of McCarthyist fascists, and that she had always wanted to sleep with an African prince, but she had never done it because she didn't know any African princes. I told her about Ola Fashola, an African prince who had sat next to me in Political Science 201, and about other legends of the American Midwest in the early 1950s.

As soon as we arrived in Vienna she dashed off saying she had to make an important phone call, her long blonde hair trailing in her wake. I put my foot on top of her suitcase and looked around the station not feeling half as foolish as I usually do coming to a strange city. I mean, here I was in Vienna, right? But I was actually waiting for someone this time, and she wasn't married or anything. Much. When she returned her face was no longer flushed with her usual flush of excitement. "Damn," she muttered. I waited for her to go on, but she just stood there muttering and scowling. So after a while I asked her if she wanted a little chow.

"I'd love some," she said, looking up and smiling. "I'm sorry I was pissed, I just had a disappointing call, that's all. I'll survive." She took my arm and off we went. Then we came back and checked our bags. A few minutes later we were outside the Westbahnhof, getting onto a number 4 bus. "This'll take us down to the Praterstern," she announced. "There's a great little restaurant there. Roast boar is their specialty. It's called Der Tiger."

"What, the boar or the restaurant?"

"Stop trying to be funny," she replied. "Where are you staying?"

"Who knows?"

"I don't have a place, either."

"I thought you had everything set up?"

"I thought so, too. Oh well. Everyone's gone on and left me again. It was my own fault, so *macht nichts.*"

"Where did you learn such good GI Deutsch?"

"From GIs, where do you think? Heidelberg is crawling with GIs."

"I know, but I didn't think students there had anything to do with them."

"As a general rule we don't. But I've been known to make an occasional and disappointing exception."

As the bus wound through the center of Vienna, Lynn pointed out all the important sights to me, like which girls were prosties and which weren't, then we got down close to the Prater and saw the lights of the Riesenrad, that huge ferris wheel they used in the movie *The Third Man.* We got off the bus there, then walked back up a little to the restaurant. I think we were the only ones in the place and I was sure the owner had an idea of closing up, but Lynn squeezed my arm and said it was OK, that no one cared how late we stayed. So we ordered chow—roast boar, naturally—and it turned out to be all right even if it did taste a little like the ham we had at the unit mess hall.

"Stop eating like a GI," she ordered halfway through the meal. So I changed hands and tried to eat in the European manner, and this seemed to please her 'cause after that all she did was smile at me.

So, everything considered, including the bottle of wine, we had a very pleasant meal. At least we didn't come to actual blows about anything. After chow we decided to head out to this other place she knew about and do a little additional drinking of a more serious nature. We—meaning I—settled the bill, then rode on a couple of strassenbahn out to the new place, which was way out, God knows where, right across from a theater—the Volksoper or someplace.

"A lot of actors and people like that hang out here," Lynn whispered to me as we sat at a small wooden table.

"Big deal."

"What's the matter, don't you like actors and people like that?"

"They're all phonies, you know that."

"Sure, so what? But they're such interesting phonies. You didn't really play football, did you?"

"Sure I did."

"Why?"

"Why what?"

"Why did you play football?"

I shrugged and took a sip of the wine which our waiter had very thoughtfully delivered to our table. "I don't know," I said. "Because it was there, I guess."

"Stop trying to be funny. Personally, I think only phony football players major in math." She smiled away at me like anything. I poured myself some more wine.

"You got that all wrong," I said, signaling the waiter for

another jug of white wine. I never really dug red wine. Red wine always made me think of spaghetti or church. "You got that all wrong," I repeated. "It's only phony math majors who play football."

After a while Lynn and I started talking about the various interesting aspects of our life histories, which, I'm sure, people imbibing as much white wine as we were are wont to do, as they say. Lynn seemed to do most of the talking, however. I don't know, it seems to me that the people who want to talk the most about their troubles are the people who don't really give a damn in the long run. I know Chuck never ever talked about his troubles to anyone. I mean, if he had something bugging him, he wasn't about to burden someone else with it. If he couldn't carry the load alone, he wouldn't . . . Oh, hell, Chuck would have kept it to himself no matter what happened. He was just that kind of guy.

"So, do you want to hear about my marriage or don't you?"

I didn't answer and pretended that I was carefully savoring the ecstatic bouquet of the wine.

"I mean, you don't have to hear about it if you don't really want to."

"It's OK," I said. "I know all about married women."

"I bet you do. I just *bet* you do." Lynn waved a finger at me, then toyed with her glass. "OK, you don't want to hear about it."

"I don't really care."

"But what do you really *want?*"

I was truthful again. "Some more wine."

"Hmmmmmm," she giggled. "You're trying to get Mummy smashed."

I was going to tell her that her name wasn't Mummy, but I saw the waiter and gave him the high sign instead. Then I stared in the general direction of her left ear.

"Why are you looking at my ear?"

"It's sexy," I replied.

"Jesus," she exclaimed. "Don't tell me you have an ear fetish or something?"

"What's that?"

"What's what?"

"An ear fetish."

"You know what it is."

I shook my head. The waiter brought us another jug. "So," I stated. "Tell me about your marriage."

"I thought you'd never ask," she giggled. Then she stared down at the table for a few minutes to get into the proper serious mood. "Well," she said, looking up finally. "It started back in college. I quit school after my junior year to marry this guy, Herbie, my husband."

I held up my hand. "Which college?"

"Colorado. Boulder. It's out past Kansas."

"I know where Colorado is."

"Yes," she said. "I believe you would. You're the type of person who would know where Colorado is."

I poured her some more wine, then waited until she continued. "So, anyway," she went on, after a few moments. "Herbie and I got married after my junior year of college. He had just graduated. He was a lousy theological student. Jesus, can you imagine me marrying a theological student?"

"I didn't know they had pre-theos at Colorado."

"He was chaplain of the ski patrol," she said, winking at me.

"I've heard all about Tulagi's," I stated. "It's out past Kansas."

"Very funny. Anyway, we fell in love and got married. Boy, did my folks ever hate that. They're Episcopalitans."

"Episcopalians."

"Who cares, they didn't like Herbie anyway."

"Why not?"

"Who knows, they just didn't like him that's all. They tried to talk me out of marrying him and everything. You know, if they just wouldn't have fought so hard against old Herbie, if they'd of encouraged me just *one* bit, the whole thing might have ended right then and there. But all they did was fight it, so I fought, too. We got married in the campus chapel about two or three minutes after he graduated. My folks didn't even come to it. You know why they didn't come? They didn't come 'cause I asked them not to, that's why. That's pretty awful, isn't it?"

"I don't know the situation," I said.

"I just explained it to you. Anyway, Herbie was accepted at theological school in Chicago and so off to Chicago we went. We had a honeymoon up along Lake Michigan, in Wisconsin someplace. You know where Wisconsin is, don't you?"

"Up along Lake Michigan someplace."

She giggled and nodded. "So we went ahead and had a great honeymoon. I mean it was really terrific."

"Look," I interrupted. "You don't have to tell me everything."

"Look, I want to tell you everything, OK?"

"OK."

"So, the honeymoon was great, really great. I mean when we had been back at Boulder a few of the kids used to tell me that pre-theos sometimes had strange ideas about some things, but they were just jealous 'cause Herbie was a pretty great guy."

"And you lived happily ever after."

"Look, if we had lived happily ever after I wouldn't be here. What happened was, we moved down to Chicago and everything turned into piss."

"Piss?"

"That's right. 'Cause you know what happened? I'll tell you what happened. I knew I was going to have to work and all that. I mean, we didn't have much money and Herbie's schooling came first. Fine. There was nothing wrong with that at all. I didn't even want to finish school. What happened was, though, was that when I got this stupid job Herbie stopped sleeping with me. I don't think he liked the idea that I was the big breadwinner and all."

"So why didn't you quit?"

"If I quit we wouldn't have had any money. I mean, he wasn't exactly a celibate, but I was lucky if maybe once or twice a month he was philosophically up to it."

"Well, how did he spend all his time then?"

"Studying, how do you think? I mean, I wasn't supporting a goddam ignoramus or anything. I think he was the world's greatest studier."

I thought for a moment. "Couldn't you . . . I mean, aren't there ways for a beautiful young woman to work things out?"

She blew some air through her nose, then looked down at the table for a moment. "Sure, sure. You know what he told me? He told me that we'd work everything out once he got ordained. Good deal, huh? And he also said he didn't want me touching him anymore when he was asleep, and you don't believe me, do you?"

"What?"

"You don't believe all this, do you?"

"Sure, I believe it."

"Then why did you just make that face?"

"I don't know," I said. "I just can't imagine sleeping in the same bed with someone and not touching, that's all."

She toyed with her wine glass. "I couldn't either," she replied softly. "Especially since things had gone so great during the honeymoon, and back at Boulder. I mean, before we got to Chicago he was a real tiger. I think, maybe, he was trying to atone for past sins and secretly hated me because I had slept with him before we were married."

"I don't believe that."

"You know Herbie?" I shook my head and smiled craftily at her. "Then how do you know?" she asked.

"I don't know. I just don't understand, I guess."

She nodded. "I never really understood either. I mean, sex isn't everything, but when it goes wrong it sure doesn't help matters any, you know what I mean?"

"I know what you mean."

"*What* do I mean?"

That stopped me. I hated to have my bluff called like that. "You're talking about the relationship of sex to successful marriages."

"You sound just like the goddam *Reader's Digest*."

"I'm trying to explain. I mean, sooner or later you have to find other things to do besides just sex. . . ."

"Right," Lynn answered. "We knew all that stuff. But I didn't think it would be a problem so soon. I mean, what you said before about being in the same bed and not touching, it's no fun let me tell you."

"So why didn't you get two beds?"

"Very funny. I didn't want them. Besides, we didn't have enough money anyway. Every once in a while, though—usually just after a big exam—Herbie would lose his head and want a little action." She stopped and smiled at me. "You look jealous."

I laughed. "I'm not jealous." Why should I be jealous? I hardly even knew her. And she hardly ever did It.

"God," she said, finishing off her glass of wine. "You're going to have to carry me home. Hey, we better start trying to find a place to stay, shouldn't we?"

"Plenty of time," I answered. "What happened then?"

"Where was I?"

"Herbie was making occasional forays."

She scowled at her glass, then touched the side of the table with her finger. "I even tried to get pregnant, but he was always one step ahead of me. I really don't know what the matter with him was. I think he could have used a psychiatrist, I really do, but you just can't go around suggesting to the top theological student in his class to see an analyst, can you? Can you?"

"I don't know," I admitted impartially.

"Well, *I* think he should have seen a psychiatrist, I really do. Anyway, one Sunday afternoon we finally had a big talk and I cried and told him what had been bugging me all along, and you know what he said? He said, let's go out for dinner tonight. Can you beat that? I mean he actually thought he was doing me a big favor."

I couldn't help it, but I had to laugh. So I did. "And *then* you lived happily ever after."

"Don't laugh at me," she said.

"I'm not laughing at you."

"The trouble with men is they never listen to you." She looked at me closely. "You sure you're really a football player?"

"That's what they told me."

"That's good," she replied, setting her glass onto the wooden table. "Anyway, I got around to leaving him on our third reunion, I mean anniversary. Then I went back home to Rochester and lived with my folks for a while. Rochester's in New York. Then my Dad sent me over here. I don't know." She looked sadly down at the table.

"What did your folks think about it?"

"They were sick, I mean really sick. Especially when Herbie went down to Mexico and got a quickie divorce. I wonder if being divorced hurts your career as a minister? Anyway, when I found out I was finally free I felt great, but my folks were absolutely sick cause it went against the good word of the Episcopal Church."

"What did they want?"

"Who knows? They wanted me to leave Herbie, but they didn't want the divorce."

"The Episcopal Church was founded on divorce," I said.

"Exactly, but who knows that today? What church do you go to?"

"I don't go to any anymore."

"What are you, an agnostic or something?"

"I don't know what you mean."

"You *are* an agnostic."

"No, I'm not," I said. "I just don't believe in going to church."

"What do you believe in?"

"Who knows?" I answered. "Steve Canyon. The Lone Ranger. John Wayne. Who knows?"

"I know what you mean," she said, nodding her head. "Personally my sympathies lie with Buddhism, but emotionally I'm a little bit Jewish."

"How can you be a little bit Jewish?"

"I don't know, I just hate Christians so goddam much it isn't funny. They're all a big bunch of phonies, you know? What they should have done was to let Christ live, then Christianity would have died a natural death."

"Oh, come on."

"No, I'm not kidding. That's where they made their big mistake. They made a martyr out of a second-rate carpenter, and you think I'm terrible, don't you?"

"No, I don't. He lived happily ever after, didn't He?"

She giggled. "Yes, you do. You think I'm absolutely terrible. The real trouble with the Jews is, though, that they need a Pope to tell them what to do."

I signaled the waiter for the check. I mean, what else was I going to do with all this talk about marriage and religion? It was getting late, and weren't we *ever* going to work out sleeping arrangements for the evening?

"I agree with you on one thing," I said. "Christianity needs a boot in the rear."

"That's not all it needs."

"I mean, where would you find a good Christian martyr today?"

"Most hypocritical religion in the world."

I looked at her for a few moments. "Are you really going over to that border tomorrow?"

"Sure," she answered. "If I find my friends. Change your mind?"

"Maybe," I said. "As long as I'm here I might as well see it. Maybe they'll need a good left guard or something."

"May*be*," she laughed. "So, what are we going to do now?"

"I don't know, Marty, what do you want to do now?"

"It's up to you, Tiger."

I smiled. "If I make the decision the decision will be that we wind up in some unreligious hotel room."

"Promise?"

"I promise."

"OK," she announced. "Make the decision."

"Look," I argued. "Don't call my bluff. I'm all hot to trot."

"So am I." she said, giggling just a bit. "Don't you think I'm terrible?"

"Huh uh," I said, waving to the waiter again.

"I've said some terrible things."

"So?"

After I paid the bill she started to giggle again.

"What's the matter?" I asked.

"I think I'll become a nun," she said.

"You're a little overtrained, aren't you?"

"What do you mean by that?"

"I don't know."

She giggled again. "I'm not *that* overtrained."

We walked outside and Lynn rested her head up against my shoulder. "I think we're going to like each other in bed," she whispered.

"There are other things besides sex," I whispered back.

She looked at me. "Why did you say that?"

"I don't know, I was trying to be funny."

"We couldn't do much there tonight anyway," she murmured.

"Where couldn't we do much?"

"At the border. Hungary."

"Oh," I said. "Oh, yeah."

She jumped away from me and waved her fist suddenly into the air. "So, let's go!" she cried out. "Let's go!"

So we went and found a hotel. Only first we had to go back to the Westbahnhof and get our bags. Then we asked a taxi driver to pick us out a place to stay, preferably unreligious. He took us someplace downtown—not too big, not too small—and we managed to get a room with no sweat, even if the names on my ID and Lynn's passport did not correspond exactly. The old man behind the counter didn't even seem to notice anything peculiar. He didn't notice that I wrote in "left guard" as my occupation, either. Lynn did, though. "Smart ass," she whispered to me, giggling again.

So we got up to the room and stared at the big, lumpy bed for a while. But not too long. "I have to see a man about a horse," she said, standing first on one foot, and then on the other.

"OK."

"You don't hate me for going to the johnny, do you?"

"Huh uh."

"I mean I'm not being very romantic and all."

I sat down on the bed and tested the springs. They were noisy. "We're not married," I said.

"Yes, isn't it great?"

She walked over to me and kissed me on the top of my head. "Mamie Eisenhower wouldn't approve," she whispered. "But then Mamie Eisenhower isn't here."

I pointed toward the door. "Go do your business," I ordered. "Do not take a ride on the Reading."

"I'm off," she announced, jumping out the door.

I took the bedspread off the bed, turned back the top sheet, then took off my shoes. I sat there for a moment, wondering how badly my feet smelled, when she returned.

"Your turn," she announced happily.

I picked up my AWOL bag and went down the hall. When I came back to the room I knocked on the door before going in.

"Who is it?" she asked.

"The house dick," I said.

"Very funny," she answered.

The lights were off. I locked the door five or six times, then hung up my clothes.

"Hurry," Lynn whispered from the bed. "Mummy's waiting."

Mummy didn't have to wait very long at all.

4

We both started to giggle when I climbed into the big, lumpy bed. Lynn was lying on her stomach, her head resting on top of one pillow. "Rub my back?" she asked.

"OK," I answered as casually as was possible under the circumstances, reaching over and starting to massage her warm back. Somehow it seemed real nice and relaxed, lying there next to her in the sack. Everything was pretty much all right, you know what I mean?

Lynn turned her head a little and snuggled a bit into the pillow. "Anytime you need a job, sweetie, you can always rub backs for a living."

"OK, sweetie."

"You don't like being called that, huh?"

"Huh uh."

"Why?"

"I sort of like my own name, you know? All this sweetie-honey-sugah crap is for the birds."

"Well, when you're—oh, I like that, right there—when you're living with someone it seems kind of monotonous calling him by his real name all the time."

"Why's that?"

She snuggled a little further down into the pillow. "I don't know," she whispered. "It just is." I rubbed her back for a while silently. "Pete?" she asked.

"I'm here."

"Hey," she whispered.

"What?"

"Getting impatient? Getting horny?"

"They're my middle names."

She giggled, then turned over on her side and put one arm around my neck. "You want me to be romantic, don't you? You want me to be a sweet little romantic girl, and all that jazz, huh?"

"Huh uh."

She smiled at me. "You should have just jumped me as soon as we got into the room. You should never have let me start talking."

"There will be an end to this interesting conversation very shortly, I have a feeling."

"Promise?" She smiled at me for a few moments, then rubbed my shoulder. "This is nice. How many times have you done it?"

"I don't know."

"Can't count that high?"

"It hasn't been that many."

"Don't get mad."

"I'm not mad. This would be a fine place to get mad."

Lynn touched my nose with her finger. "More people are mad in bed than out of bed."

"Don't give me any of that."

"Whatever you say, *sweetie*."

"And none of that, either."

She giggled. "Seriously, very few people are completely satisfied in bed."

"Listen," I said. "Sex isn't everything. Some people can hold hands and be completely satisfied."

"Let's hold hands," she chuckled. "God, you sound just like Norman Vincent Peale."

"That's a terrible thing to say." She smiled up at me as I smiled down. And it was pretty nice lying there in that huge, lumpy sack feeling her warm, naked legs up against mine one moment, then far away the next, and watching her giggle and laugh, and hearing the whispering rustle of the sheets.

I reached my foot out and touched hers. Our toes played with each other for a while, and then our knees bumped. Lynn turned toward me and, for a very brief second, put her tongue into my ear. It felt as if someone had poured in a warm, ticklish dose of honey. She leaned back and looked at me. "Like that, GI?"

"Yeah," I answered hoarsely. "That felt just like a warm, ticklish dose of honey."

And then, all of a sudden, we seemed mighty close to each other. I ran my finger down her back and came back up over her arm. Lynn looked right at me, her eyes as half-closed as mine were. My finger circled her shoulder and zigzagged across her neck. She leaned back a little, then completely closed her eyes. Our legs became rather tightly ensnarled. My finger rested against her neck for a second, then traversed back to her shoulder and slowly down her arm. She started to frown a little and so I smiled at her left ear, as my finger reached the small of her back, then started the slow, delightful trip north-by-northeast. Very lightly, very softly it continued up her fuzzy stomach, then circled each breast—very, very slowly.

Suddenly, she pushed away from me. "God," she whimpered. "Stop teasing me."

"What do you mean?"

"You know what I mean."

I laughed at her not-too-angry manner. Somehow it made her seem almost twice as sexy. Our toes began to play eeny-meeny-miny-moe again. "There is an old Oriental proverb," I whispered. "That he who takes long time has long fun."

"Big deal," she growled. "Well, stop being so goddam Oriental then. Orientals don't give a hot damn about their women anyway."

"Sure they do."

"No, they don't." She pulled away from me and looked under the sheet. "Yours isn't such long fun anyway."

"Take another look," I laughed. We both laughed. "You ever read *The Brothers Karamazov?*" I asked.

"What would I read that for?"

"We had to. Old man Karamazov—he was some guy. He said the sack was his battlefield and that's where he wanted to die."

"Yeah? Maybe I should read it after all."

"It's about the only thing I remember about that book." It was, too.

I smiled at her again, and before she could smile back we were both kissing. It's funny, but that was the first time we had actually kissed. I could feel something sort of flutter around in her stomach and I was going to break off the kiss and tell her that, but I changed my mind and didn't. I did open my eyes and look at her, but closed them when she didn't look back. Pretty soon I felt hands running up and down my back, and pretty soon my hands were holding her back tightly, and then, pretty soon, we were as close as two people could get to each other. My hands crept up to her shoulders and I felt her hands creep up and start to play with my ears. Very slowly I dropped my left hand to the top of her left breast and caressed it gently with the back of my fingers, then lifted my hand carefully until it closed around the other soft, warm mound.

"Oh," she whispered. "Oh, God."

I gently rolled on top of her, feeling her thighs swing open for me. We kissed again, which was very nice indeed, then wrapped every arm and leg we could muster around each other.

"Oh, God, what are you waiting for?" she hissed. "What are you waiting for?"

I wasn't waiting for anything. I forced myself back for a moment, then hovered over her on my knees, then down I came—falling delightfully and eagerly into the waiting den of warmth. Lynn's hands tightened around my neck and I stuck my head into the pillow right next to her left ear.

"Oh, yes," she said as the train started to pull out of the station and go into motion. "Oh, yes."

Slowly, very slowly, the train moved. It was going to be a local, with lots of starts and jolts and slow, coasting curves. I was determined it was going to be a local. But someone had fiddled with the throttle. The train started up and ran right out of control. I bypassed a lot of good stations. We roared around the curves. Suddenly, I was off the track.

"Oh."

"Just a sec."

"There."

Everything was all right again. I slowed the train down.

"Slowly," someone whispered. "Slowly."

But the train just didn't want to go slowly. I tried to catch my breath and go slow, but everything went out of control again. It kept moving, and moving, and moving . . . And the fires were burning; the fires were burning! God, it was hot . . . So damn hot! . . . Come on, train. Come on, train . . . Come on . . .

Off in the blurred grayness of the pillow I saw a bright sun waiting for me, waiting for me. It was far off, but it was getting larger and larger, nearer and nearer. I was conscious of the engine huffing and puffing and gasping for air. I could hear its echo right next to my ear. "Oh, yes," it hissed. "Oh, yes."

The sun was jumping up and down now, up and down. The pillow was suffocating me with its bouncing heat.

"Wonderful . . ." the echo hissed. "Oh, wonderful . . ."

The train was racing, racing, racing, racing. And there was the sun. There was the sun! I could see some spots on it. Spots. Black spots. They were right in front of me. I was racing up the mountain now, and the spots were right in front of me. Right there! And then I was on the top, looking down, looking down, looking down. I was pushed off the top; something pushed me off. I couldn't stop—I was going to crash. I was going to crash into the black spots. They weren't spots anymore. They had turned into a fence. A big, black fence. I couldn't slow down. I couldn't stop. I crashed. I groaned. I went down. Down, down, down.

"Not yet," someone called.

"Please not yet," a voice cried.

But I was already on the fence. There was someone next to it—someone standing there. Someone I knew.

"Steph!" someone yelled. "Steph! STEPH!"

And then the train settled into a soft cloud of laziness. I didn't care about the train anymore. I didn't care about anything anymore. I can remember desperately trying to catch my breath. I can remember swallowing about a hundred times. I remember feeling the sweat run down my back and sting where something had scratched me. Oh, God, I was hot and tired.

I felt a tapping on my back. It got louder and louder. "You came too quickly," a voice hissed in my ear. "You were too fast." It wasn't a tapping any longer, it was the pounding of small fists. I tried to crouch up on my knees, to release some of the burning pressure.

"No, please," a voice called out. "Not yet."

I tried to catch my breath. I was covered with the train's steam. I wanted to get away. I wanted to fly. I wanted to dive into a stream of cold water. I wanted to lie on my back. I wanted to be free.

I pushed back and rolled over.

"Oh, no," she whined. We both looked up at the ceiling. Everything was dark and hot and sticky. Everything was tired.

"I'm sorry," I said when my breathing had returned to normal.

She didn't answer me.

We were silent and alone.

"I'm sorry," I said again.

"Oh," she answered. "I thought you were asleep."

I shook my head. "I'm usually more Oriental."

"Look, forget it, will you? It doesn't make any difference now."

"It makes a difference to me."

We were silent again. Lynn got up out of the bed and found her cigarettes, then lit one up and lay back down. All of a sudden I didn't want to touch her at all; all of a sudden I didn't want her touching me.

I remember hearing one time—maybe I read it in my psych textbook—about this guy with a big masturbation problem. He'd gone to all this trouble of hooking up some complex electrical apparatus so that every time his pecker got hard, it would ring a bell which would wake him up so that he could go back to work on it again. The book never did say if the guy finally worked out his problem or not. I mean he probably ended up a physical wreck or something. But that's the trouble with those psych textbooks—they tell you all the problems all right, but they don't give any of the answers.

Personally I think the guy had the right idea. He was doing exactly what he wanted to do. All sorts of people were probably going around telling him he was crazy, but if that's what he wanted to do, why not just let him do it? I mean, basically, that's Americanism, right? Doing what you want to do.

These thoughts were more or less drifting around inside my overheated mind as I lay on the side of that bed, in that hotel room, somewhere in Vienna. In Austria, for crissakes.

"Sleeping?" she asked.

"Huh uh."

"What were you thinking about?"

"Nothing."
"Tell me."
I was silent. She started to slide over next to me. I turned away and faced the wall. Her arms crept around my shoulders, then slid down my arms and found my hands. Her legs rested right behind my legs.
"This is called sleeping spoon," she whispered.
"I know."
"How do you know? You've never been married."
"I know everything."
She rubbed the back of my legs with her knees. "Were you really a football player?"
"Yep."
"What position did you play?"
"I told you, I played left guard."
"Where's the left guard play?"
"Right next to the center."
"You mean you were in the line?"
"That's right."
She kicked me playfully. "I never slept with a crummy lineman before."
"I never slept with a divorced woman before."
She snorted, then put her hand on my hip. I turned my head to the pillow.
"Why'd you move?"
"You know."
"Was he coming to attention?"
"That he was."
"Embarrassed?"
"Huh uh!"
"Then why'd you move?"
I put the pillow over my head and my hands over the pillow. She started to massage my back, very slowly. "You like this, GI?" she asked.

"Mmmmmm," I murmured. Her hands slid down to the small of my back, then I could feel her knee rubbing up against the back of my thigh. Pretty soon I turned over and faced her. I mean, it certainly seemed like the logical thing to do. All of a sudden she was bent over me, her mouth nicely placed on mine. I felt her hands pressing down on my shoulders, pinning me to the bed. Then, as we kissed, her hands stole up to my face and circled my mouth.

Then she was breathing into my ear. "Just relax," she whispered. "Just relax." I relaxed as much as I could—which wasn't very much, believe me. Her hand reached back and threw off the sheet. I could feel the cool air sweeping over me, and then it was just our two little hot bodies facing the cool, gray night.

"Be very still," she whispered. I was very still. I wasn't going anyplace. Her hand reached down and touched me. At first it was gentle, but then it was hard and cruel.

"Hey," I whispered. I looked up at her, but her eyes were closed. And then she was all over me. I tried to push her back and roll over on top, but she forced me back down. I didn't fight very hard.

"Let me," she hissed. "Let *me*." She was biting her lip and then her face bent toward my ear. "Hold on, baby," she whispered. "Hold on." I held on. I was covered by a heavy warmth—and then everything began to move. We ran off the track several times, but each time she eased everything back into place. And then we were off again—jolting, bumping, racing. After a short ride she leaned back, her face all contorted. The ride became faster, rougher. It was a crushing, bouncing, hurting ride. I held on as tightly as I could, but it was hurting me, bouncing me, jolting me. And then she stopped moving and squirmed from side to side. Her head twisted back and forth, back and forth.

"God," she whispered. "God!"

I grabbed her shoulders and tried to stay onboard. She was hardly moving at all, but everything felt as if it were moving. "Oh, baby," she shouted. "Baby!"

When would it stop? When would it stop?

A bump—a shout—a crash . . . "Herbie!" someone called.

And then the train stopped. It fell on top of me. It had captured me. I didn't want to be captured. I wanted to be free. I wanted to take charge. But I heard the engine in my ear and I knew I was caught. It was too late to be free. And then finally—oh, finally—everything moved away, everything rested.

We must have fallen asleep, but I was conscious of her next to me. Sometime during the night I faintly recall a dream that I was running out onto the playing fields of Ohio again, that I was practicing away like crazy, that I was all set to go again, but then someone shouted to me that the game was over, that the game was over, that we should all roll over and sleep, that we should rest. And I remember feeling exhausted and depressed and confused—just like I had after we had lost to Michigan my junior year—but since the game was over and we had lost there was nothing else to do but sleep.

And so I slept.

When I woke up I had a headache. I got up out of bed quietly, dressed, then left the room. Lynn was curled up underneath the sheet and didn't seem to notice. I walked the streets of Vienna for about an hour. I bought a paper from an old man and tried to read what was happening in Budapest. As best as I could make out the Russians had returned to the city and had once again taken control. There was another story about the UN and Suez, but I couldn't translate the real gist of it. I didn't try too hard. So I stuffed the paper into my coat pocket, then listened to the chiming of some church bells in the very near vicinity. The thumping in the back of my head kept hollow time.

I walked back to the hotel and found an old woman in the kitchen, listening to the news on a battered old radio. "*Wie geht der Putsch?*" I asked.

She didn't understand. I couldn't think of the right words. I pointed to the radio. "*Wie geht's?*"

"*Alles ist kaputt,*" the old woman croaked.

I nodded and tried to make out what the announcer was saying. What he was saying wasn't good, that much I could tell. The old woman asked what my room number was. When I told her she smiled and gave me a tray with coffee and rolls. My headache was getting worse.

I carried the tray upstairs and walked right into the room without knocking. She was still in bed.

"Ummmm?" Lynn mumbled, turning over underneath the covers.

"Chowtime," I said.

A fuzzy blonde head poked out from around the end of a sheet. "What?"

"Breakfast."

"Oh," she replied, running a hand through her hair. "What time is it?"

"About ten thirty," I said, sliding the table closer to the bed.

Lynn yawned, then snuggled down under the covers, leaving just her head free. "Where did you go?"

"Out." I poured her some coffee and handed it to her.

"Thanks." She sipped it for a while, then looked at me. "How do you feel?"

"OK. How do you feel?"

She set the cup and saucer on the bed. "Not too awfully bad." She yawned again, then brushed her hair back with one hand.

"The Russians are back in Budapest," I said. "Their tanks went in during the night."

"How do you know?"

"I got a paper. They have it on the radio downstairs."

"Oh," she answered. "Hand me my slip, will you?"

I looked around the room and found her slip hanging in the closet, then handed it to her. She put it on in bed, then held out her cup for a refill. "Now," she stated. "What I need is a cigarette." I must have scowled or something, 'cause she asked what was that for?

"What was what for?"

"That look. Don't you like smoking?"

"I can't understand how people can smoke first thing in the morning."

"Why not? I've had some coffee."

"I don't know."

She lit up a Gauloise, then smiled at me. "When I was first married I used to get up early and brush my teeth."

"What for?"

"So I'd taste sweet and pretty for my good-morning kiss."

"Was that before or after the honeymoon?"

"Don't be bitter."

"I'm not bitter." I wasn't bitter about anything. Not much. "Got a headache," I said.

She took a bite out of a roll then reached over and touched my hand. "Poor baby. Everyone should have breakfast in bed. You think I'm sexier in a slip or just plain naked?"

I finished my coffee and looked at the opposite wall. "You look pretty sexy either way."

"You didn't answer the question."

"What difference does it make?"

"I want to know. I don't have very big boobs."

"So?"

"So, some people have a big boob complex and all. All they live and die for is big boobies."

I grinned at her in spite of my headache. "You know the sexiest girl I've ever seen?" I asked. "It was this nutty girl I was going with in college. I stayed at her home once between semesters and one time, when her folks were out, she wanted me to take a shower with her."

"That's great," Lynn said. "Herbie liked all that exotic crap, too."

"What's so exotic about taking a shower?"

"Nothing. But it's a start, right?"

"Well," I admitted. "I didn't do it though."

"Why not?"

"I was only in college at the time, I didn't know any better." Lynn laughed then waited for me to go on. "Anyway, she took a shower, though, and when she came out she had this pink, furry towel wrapped all around her. That was the sexiest thing I've ever seen."

"Did she have big boobs?"

I shook my head. "Great legs, though."

"I have great legs. Did you screw her?"

I choked on the coffee, so I set my cup down. "Huh uh. Everyone thought I did, but I didn't."

"Why not?"

"I don't know. I thought at one time I might marry her."

"So?"

"So, I don't know." I didn't know, either. I think I was scared I might make her pregnant and then have to quit the team. Her old man was heartbroken we broke up, but actually I think he was more heartbroken I didn't make it with the Browns. Well, it broke my heart, too, but not for the same reason. "You want some more coffee?" I asked.

Lynn shook her head, then yawned again, sliding down beneath the covers just a bit. I took her cup and put it onto the table, then took off my shoes and lay down next to her.

"Why don't you climb in with me?"

"Nah."

"Toasty warm in here."

"OK." I didn't really want to get back under the covers with her, but then I couldn't think of any real reason not to, either. So I sat on the edge of the bed and took off my sweater and pants, then swung my legs underneath. Lynn moved over next to me right away.

"This is nice," she whispered. "Let's stay in bed all day."

"We're going to the border, aren't we?"

"We don't have to."

"I thought you wanted to."

"Ummmmmmm," she murmured. "Let's not talk about it now, OK? I mean it's still morning, isn't it?" Suddenly she started to giggle. "This is a funny bed."

I nodded and looked up at the ceiling. The drum in the back of my head was getting louder, stronger. Lynn put her hands on my temples and started to massage them.

"Don't," I said.

"Bad headache?"

"Yeah," I replied.

Her hands went underneath the covers and tickled one thigh. "Is this the one you broke?"

"The other one." Her fingers tripped across to the other leg.

"You really do have a headache, don't you?"

"I guess I do."

Her hands stopped playing around. "Well," she announced. "A good workman always cleans his tool." Then she bounced up out of bed, slipped into my coat, and padded out of the room in her bare feet. I still looked up at the ceiling, trying hard not to move a throbbing muscle. She came back a few minutes later. "Hey," she said, dropping the paper I had bought onto the bed. "You were right."

Big deal. I was aware of her opening a suitcase and then brushing her long blonde hair furiously. She lit another cigarette in a moment, then went back to work on her hair.

"Do you have to smoke?" I asked.

"Does it bother you, sweetie?" she replied, looking at my reflection in the mirror.

"It's getting a little stuffy."

She stopped brushing and jumped back into bed. "Then open the window." She took the paper and rustled through its noisy pages.

"Can't you do that a little quieter?"

"Do what?"

"Turn the pages."

She didn't answer. She folded the newspaper in half and studied one story intently. "The Security Council recessed until tomorrow," she said. "The Russians claim they don't know anything about their tanks surrounding Budapest. That's a big laugh."

"I read it."

"What?"

"I said I already read it."

"Oh," she answered, rustling the pages some more. "Sorry."

I closed my eyes and tried to concentrate on stopping the constant throbbing in the back of my head.

"Do you think the UN should do something?" she asked.

I didn't answer. What the hell did I care about the UN? Chuck had been killed fighting for the UN. After a while, Lynn sighed and lay back down on the bed. I sat up and started to rustle through the pages of the paper.

"Stop making so much noise," she said, turning away from me.

All of a sudden I laughed. "Hey," I said. "We're acting pretty silly."

"*You're* acting pretty silly."

"Come on," I said, touching her arm. "Let's get up and go to the border."

"I'm getting a headache," she said.
"Oh, Jesus."
"Look, do you mind not swearing like that?"
"Like what?"
"Never mind."
I got off the bed, put my clothes back on and shoved my shaving gear into my bag. I looked into the mirror for a second and saw her looking back at me from the bed. "I'm leaving."
"Goodbye."
I picked up my bag and walked to the door. I opened it, looked outside, then closed it with a bang. She sat up abruptly on the bed. "Wait!" she called out. And then she saw me standing there, laughing silently at her. "You bastard," she giggled.
I laughed out loud, dropped my bag onto the floor, then walked over to her. "Scared I left, huh?"
She pulled the sheet up around her. "Get away from me," she hissed. "I have a headache."
I stared down at her for a while, smirking.
"What are you smirking about?"
"You."
"Well, stop it, you make me nervous."
"You love every smirking minute of it."
"Screw you, sweetie." She slipped one leg out of bed, then the other. She padded over to the mirror and looked at herself. "God, what a witch." She picked up the brush and went to work on her hair again.
"So let's go to the border," I said.
"You really want to go, don't you?"
"Sure," I said, staring at her slip. "That's why we came, wasn't it?"
"I don't know," she mumbled, brushing her long, blonde hair like anything. "Do you mind if I don't wear a bra?"
"I don't care."

" 'Cause if there's one thing I hate—it's wearing bras and girdles."

"That's two things."

"I mean, everyone would be a lot happier if they didn't wear all this crap, you know? That's why American women are so frustrated, basically they're uncomfortable."

I laughed, but only a little.

Then she dropped her brush, turned and looked at me. "The hell with it," she said. "I'm going back to bed." Then she lunged across the floor before I could stop her and dived underneath the covers. " 'Bye," she called out.

"Come on, Lynn," I urged. "We came here to go to the border, didn't we?"

"I came, you just followed."

"Who paid your way?"

"*Macht nichts.* We couldn't do anything anyway now that the Russians have come back." She looked at me. "You want me to pay you back?"

"Huh uh."

"Then why did you bring it up?"

"Bring what up?"

"Forget it."

"So, let's go," I said, forgetting it.

"I'm not going."

"But why?"

She sat up and reached for a cigarette. After she had it lit, and had readjusted the pillows behind her back, she looked in my general direction. "Why do you want to go to the border? You didn't have the hots to go yesterday."

"I don't know," I admitted softly. "Maybe, all of a sudden, I'm feeling guilty about a lot of things."

"Like what? Don't tell me you feel guilty about last night?"

"No, I don't feel guilty about that. I don't know. Forget it."

"Ho ho ho," she declared. "Someone's getting testy."

"Look . . ."

She shook her head. "I think you're just making some grandstand play because you have a headache."

"Look," I said, my voice getting a little louder. "I feel guilty because my brother got killed in Korea while I was running around playing football."

"What's that have to do with us? With going to the border?"

"Nothing. You wouldn't understand."

She smiled. "You hate me, don't you?"

How could I hate her, I hardly even knew her? "What?"

She nodded. "Yes, you really hate me. You're probably just another one of those phony Christians. Scratch a phony and you'll find a Christian."

"I think you have me confused with someone else."

"What?"

"Nothing." I picked up my bag, then set it down. "Look, are you going to the border or aren't you?"

"I'm not going with you, that's for sure."

"OK," I said. "OK."

"Jack Armstrong, the All American Boy," she scoffed. "Who's this Steph?"

"Who?"

She blew some smoke at me, nodding violently. "Uh huh. Uh huh. One if by land, two if by sea."

"What are you talking about?"

"What the hell kind of name is Steph, anyway? She one of your Schatzies? That chick back home? . . . Huh?" Her eyes narrowed. "You're just a phony Christian bastard, you know that?"

I must have started to raise my hand 'cause she flinched.

"Go ahead," she shouted. "That's the Christian thing to do, isn't it? Huh? Isn't it?"

My arm dropped. I looked at her, shaking my head from

side to side. "You know," I said slowly. "Maybe it wasn't your ex-husband who needed the psychiatrist, after all."

"What?" she screeched.

I didn't answer, I just picked up my bag once more. She jumped out of bed and stood right in front of me. "What do you mean by that? What do you mean?"

"Nothing."

"Look, you phony fuckin' bastard, why don't you just get the fuck out of here?!" I started for the door. "Feeling guilty about your brother?" she hissed angrily. "You don't feel guilty about anything. You're just a fuckin' phony American bastard . . . Go on, get out of . . . here!"

I turned and looked at her. If I had known what to say I would have said it, but I didn't know what to say so I hit her. She wheeled around and fell back against the bed. "Get out, get out, get out," she sobbed.

I got out. What else was I going to do?

5

The sky was still gray, but somehow it didn't seem half as depressing as before. Maybe it was just because my headache had gone away. Maybe it was because I was in the town of Eisenstadt, about forty miles east of Vienna, and about twelve Ks west of the Hungarian border. We always called kilometers "klicks" or "Ks."

I walked through the streets of Eisenstadt and saw people coming out of churches, all dressed in somber black suits. I passed a large, castlelike church and saw a small sign saying that it was where Haydn was entombed. I walked around seeing everything until I got hungry and found a small gasthaus and went in and ordered some oxtail soup and some cheese. And then I thought about what had happened.

After I had left Lynn and the hotel I had walked through the center of Vienna, looking at all the buildings and dodging the traffic. Then I walked past the big opera house and soon found myself standing right in front of the American Express office. Big deal. The place was closed, of course, but there was a map of Austria in the window and so I picked out Eisenstadt as a likely city to head for. I grabbed a strassenbahn to the Sudbahnhof, then found the bus depot right next door. I had to wait almost an hour and a half for a bus to Eisenstadt and I spent the entire time thinking about the night before. I thought of trying to call back to the hotel and apologizing to Lynn, but then I remembered that there wasn't any phone in our room. I didn't really want to apologize anyway. If it hadn't been for Lynn and the night before I wouldn't have been on my way to the border. And that's where I wanted to go.

The bus passed through such well-known towns as Laxenburg and Ebreichsdorf. And then, after a bumping, depressing ride, we arrived in Eisenstadt. And so I sat in the gasthaus eating my lunch, feeling completely alone and hollow. For one of the few times in my life I felt completely helpless. Exactly what the hell was I doing twelve Ks from the Hungarian border? What was I doing?

And then two men sat down at my table. I nodded to them, and they nodded back, but it depressed me even more 'cause I was sort of enjoying my lonely depression. They ordered beer and wurst, then started to converse in English. I had them pegged as Australian or Scots, but I wasn't sure. Not that it made that much difference. After a while I asked them if they were reporters. One of the men, tall and pale, sort of fiddled with his glasses before he answered me. "In a manner of speaking," he said. "We work for a travel magazine out of Toronto. And you?"

"I'm on my own," I said.

"Come to see the border?"

"That's right."

"Really some show," the other man said, looking at me over a forkful of wurst.

"Are you going to Budapest?" I asked.

Both men shook their heads. "That's one bloody city I wouldn't go close to at the moment."

I dug out my paper. "I read here where the Russians are coming back into the city. Do you know what's happened?"

The tall man with the glasses shook his head. "We listened to a broadcast from Budapest this morning. Terrible, absolutely terrible."

The other man pointed his fork at me. "They've had it, you know. It's all over now."

"But," I argued, "if they hold out until tomorrow the UN will be back in session."

"Yes!" he exclaimed. "You know what will happen in the

UN when it reconvenes? Nothing will happen, because by tomorrow this will be entirely an internal affair of the Hungarian government."

"But the Russian troops . . . ?"

"Makes no difference," the man with the glasses said. "Kadar will be back in the driver's seat—his men are at the UN. All he has to do is say that he requested Russian assistance to put down local disturbances, and then the UN hasn't a right in the world to do anything. I really think they're more concerned about Suez anyway."

"A bloody shame," the other added.

"It just doesn't seem right," I said.

"The Spanish Civil War never seemed right to me," the man with the glasses said. "Neither did World War II, really. What country has the right to do anything to another country? I'm not so sure the English and French have a right to take over Suez, but who knows? Certainly the Russians have no real right to be in Hungary, but—of course—the Russians have been there all along and no one has raised a finger to stop them."

"You see," the other man said. "The poor Hungarians couldn't have picked a worse time for a revolution. Not with Suez, and your election, and the fact that there is a bitter power struggle going on in the Kremlin." He shook his head for a moment. "That's what a lot of people are overlooking, I'm afraid. That man in the Kremlin is on pretty shaky footing, and he can't afford another Poland at the moment. So he has to send his troops back into Budapest or he might end up like his old chum Beria."

"I will say," his companion added, "that the West has lost a golden opportunity. I mean the Russians actually did leave Budapest for a while. It's just a shame that this whole business came at absolutely the worst possible time."

"The *worst* possible time."

"The West had its foot in the door, but they're letting it be slammed shut."

"It's not over yet, is it?" I asked.

The man with the glasses shook his head. "If what we heard on the radio this morning is true—that Russian tanks are controlling Budapest again—then there isn't a chance in the world. Once Nagy is taken, the control will return to Kadar. And with Kadar in the driver's seat, the UN will be helpless."

I thought for a moment, then looked at the two men. "We should have sent the troops out," I stated.

"Even if it meant risking a major war?"

I nodded. "I'm beginning to think so."

"Well," he replied thoughtfully. "Truman sent the troops into Korea, even before he had UN sanction. He didn't exactly defeat the other side, but he got there soon enough to show them he wasn't going to be pushed around."

"It's too late though, now," the other man said.

We were all silent for a few minutes. "Are you writing a story on all this?" I asked.

They both chuckled. "No," the man with the glasses said. "After our discussion it hardly seems fair to tell him what we're actually doing here, doesn't it, Paul?"

Paul grinned at me. "We're doing a picture story on eastern Austria. We took some shots of Haydn's church this morning. This afternoon we plan to go up to one of those towns along the Neusiedler See where the storks live in the chimneys of the houses. Have you ever seen them?"

I shook my head. "I just came to Vienna for the first time last night."

"Where are you headed?"

"I'm not exactly sure," I admitted. "I wanted to go to the border. I wanted to see what was going on. I don't know, I just wanted to be there, I guess."

Paul looked at his companion. "We might as well see one of those crossing points ourselves," he said.

"Would you like to go with us as far as Nicklesdorf?" the man with the glasses asked.

"Actually," Paul said. "We don't have to go as far as Nicklesdorf—there's a crossing point closer, I believe."

They both looked at me. "OK with me," I said.

So we went to the border.

Driving there we got to talking about Korea. I let them do most of the talking. I mean, I had absolutely nothing to say about Korea. Not after what had happened to Chuck. I mean, we settled for a tie in Korea. A tie! God, that was the worst possible thing we could have done. My old man thought we should have bombed Manchuria, but I don't know about that. What pissed me off most was the Big General saying that he'd go to Korea to shape things up. He shaped things up all right—he shaped them up by settling for a tie. When I'd been a junior in high school we had an open date one Saturday and the whole varsity had been invited up to West Point to see Army play. The game was tied in the last quarter and Army had a chance to go ahead, but instead of taking a chance on a possible win, the cadets had played it cozy and made sure of a certain tie. Boy, I tell you, old Crazy Ed almost went out of his mind. Smokey would have gone out of his mind, too. If Smokey had been in charge of Korea he never would have settled for a tie.

"They could have been bluffed," Paul was saying. "They were bluffed in Korea, they could have been bluffed in Hungary."

"Maybe it's not too late," I said.

They shook their heads. "Too late," they mumbled. "Too late."

And also an election year.

We drove down a one-lane road until it stopped in the

middle of a field. To one side were about twenty cars, buses, and ambulances. On the other side of the road a line of tents had been set up. The Red Cross sign was on one tent. I don't know, some of the guys back at the unit griped like anything about the Red Cross—especially when they had to pay for their own coffee and doughnuts out in the field—but the Red Cross had never bothered me, so I never bothered them.

We got out of the car and walked up to the crossing. About fifteen people were standing there, looking out across the field. Half of the group were in some sort of uniform, and most of them were looking through binoculars. To the left of the road, about fifty yards in front of us, was a tall, wooden tower. Sloping down from the tower was a long, large field, stretching out almost as far as I could see. Between the tower and where we were standing was a patch of marshy ground, then farther down to the left was a clump of small trees, and then—blending into the scene—was the fence. I stared at the fence for a while, then looked over at the right side of the road. There was a small rise there, covered with trees. And in the middle of the trees I could make out a continuation of the fence. Anyone traveling into Austria would have to cross over that huge field, then climb the fence; or climb up the hill, and climb the fence; or walk along the road, and go right underneath the tower. An alert guard would be able to spot anyone approaching the border, anyone at all.

Paul walked over to one of the men in uniform and talked with him for a few minutes, then returned. "Amazing," he said, shaking his head. "Only yesterday there was a steady stream of refugees coming across this road with no trouble at all. Now, only a few scattered groups are crossing. They all think it's only a question of time before the Russians return and close the border." He looked at me a moment, then pointed out toward the huge field. "You see that tractor way out there? As long as that farmer keeps the tractor plowing the people know it's safe to cross."

"How come?"

"I guess he serves as the go-ahead signal."

"But what about the tower?"

Paul shrugged. "He's a Hungarian. I wouldn't want to be in his shoes when the Russians come."

I was about to ask some more questions when suddenly there were some shouts from the group of men just next to us. They pointed just to the right of the tower. At first, I could see nothing, but then—in a few seconds—I could make out a small line of people struggling toward us. I counted eight people in the group, some carrying bundles and suitcases, others carrying nothing. No one seemed the least bit happy in reaching Austria.

A man who had been watching it all through binoculars turned to us, shaking his head. "It will not go on much longer," he said. "The Russians, they come very soon."

"How do you know?"

He nodded. "I know. They come." He smiled at us. "They come and then—poof."

"Who is in the tower now?" I asked.

He shrugged. "A Hungarian soldier. He will not stop his own people. The Russians will come and shoot him."

"And the man on the tractor?"

"He also."

"Won't they try to escape?"

The man gave me his binoculars. "Look," he said. I focused the glasses on the tractor. It was an old man driving the machine. A very old man. I swung the binoculars around and looked at the tower. The Hungarian soldier seemed to be a boy of sixteen or seventeen.

The man took back his glasses. "One very old; one very young. They never leave Hungary. They be shot."

He gestured back toward the tents. "Hungarian farmers not try to come over to Austria. Only people from the cities."

He smiled at us, tipped his hat, then walked away. I looked at my two companions. None of us said a word.

We followed the refugees back to the tents. There they were given something to eat, and then, after only a little processing, they were put on buses and driven away.

"There's a refugee camp outside of Vienna," Paul said. "If I know refugee camps they'll probably want to go right back to Hungary."

"After they've come this far?"

"Don't get me wrong," Paul replied, looking at me. "I know they must have good reasons for coming over here. But a refugee camp is still a refugee camp, no matter which side of the Iron Curtain it's on."

A few minutes later the two men agreed that they had better be moving on. They asked me if I wanted a lift any place, but I shook my head. I was alone and depressed and I wanted to stay right where I was—alone in the most depressing spot I've ever known. I didn't feel like I was ready to leave just yet.

After we had said our goodbyes, I walked around the tents, then listened to some photographers arguing with an official of some sort, demanding to be allowed to photograph the refugees as they crossed over into Austria. I guess photographers were the same the world over—always trying to take pictures of things they had no business taking pictures of. Smokey used to keep the photographers out of the locker room no matter if we won or lost. Who wanted to see pictures of people crying their eyes out? Especially when all they were crying about was losing a kid's game.

There were some more shouts from the border. Another group of people was crossing over. I rushed back to the road and stared at the sloping ground just to the left of the tower. Five people were moving slowly in our direction. They took at least ten minutes to straggle across the last fifty yards. It seemed like ten minutes anyway. The last to cross over was a girl, a girl who couldn't have been more than seventeen or eighteen. She collapsed as soon as she was on Austrian soil, falling face down onto the road. For a moment or two everyone just stared at her, then we all rushed to help. I took her arm and walked with her back to the tents. She was very pretty.

When we reached the tent she looked up at me. "*Vielen Dank,*" she whispered uncertainly, smiling in a sickly sort of way.

"You're more than welcome," I replied in English.

The small, sick smile froze on her weary, dirty face. She frowned at me, then looked away. "You are English?" she asked.

I shook my head and smiled apologetically. "American."

She looked at me for several seconds without saying a word. "American," she whispered to herself. "American."

I smiled again.

She looked at me for several more seconds, then spit right into my face.

I was too surprised to do a thing. I wanted to follow her down to the tents and talk to her, to find out why she hated me, or Americans in general. But I didn't. I just didn't know how to go about it. Besides, if I'd been in her shoes I would probably have hated Americans, too.

And then I heard the shots. They came suddenly, sharply, from the tower. They weren't fired in our direction, though; they were being fired at the tractor—the tractor driven by that old Hungarian farmer. The tractor whose tires were very shortly shot out. The Russians had arrived.

We all yelled for the old man to run. We shouted in a variety of languages. But just as he finally jumped down from his tractor, there was another burst of fire from the tower. The man spun around and fell to the ground. Christ, I thought, he's had the old schnitz now. But then I saw the small, dark figure start to crawl away from the tractor, slowly edging his way in our direction. Oh God, I whispered, he'll never make it. He'll be in range of the tower the whole time. And then he'd have to crawl through the marsh. And climb the fence.

I couldn't watch it any longer. I couldn't sit on the bench any longer. I had to do something. I had to!

I broke away from the group of people on the road. I dashed down into that huge, plowed field. I was conscious of some shouts behind me, but I couldn't hear what was being yelled. I was conscious of the tower to my right, but all of a sudden I just didn't give a good goddam.

All of a sudden, I was in Hungary.

All of a sudden, I was doing something.

Here was my chance at last to really be John Wayne.

I was loose and ready. It was like falling out of a tree. It was like diving from a high tower. It was like that moment in lovemaking when you're almost there, but not quite. It was like the moment just after you've finally made a decision.

It was a good feeling. It was a free feeling. You were falling, diving, loving, running . . . And I was loose and ready.

I remember stumbling over one of the plowed furrows, but it was like when you're running down a hill and you've worked up so much momentum that you couldn't possibly fall or stop. And I couldn't possibly stop. I was conscious of my own sounds at first, but then I noticed small clods of dirt kicking up around me. Then they were gone. And I didn't hear anything else. But I was sure people were shouting at me. . . . It was like being out on the field of Ohio Stadium—you knew all the people were there all right, and you knew they were all shouting something, but you couldn't tell what it was they were shouting.

I jumped across a small hedge, then staggered through a series of freshly plowed furrows. Where was the man? Where was he? I looked over at the tractor and swept my eyes slowly toward the fence. There he was! He was still crawling, but he had been angling away from the fence, not going toward it.

I ran over to him and fell down next to his crawling, ancient body. He didn't notice me at first, then he jumped away when I put my hand on his shoulder.

"*Komst,*" I whispered. "*Verstehen? Du komst?*" The old man looked at me with his hurting, tired eyes. And then he smiled. I don't think he understood at all. "*Wir gehen nach Oesterreich,*" I said, pointing off toward the fence. He smiled at me again, then nodded. I put my arm around his shoulder and tried to crawl with him to the fence. It was tough going. It was awfully tough going. It wasn't a ride downhill anymore. It was a slow, bitter climb. All of a sudden I was conscious of the wind blowing. And of the settling dusk. And of the clammy coldness of the plowed earth.

I was tired and out of shape. I was worried. I was no longer the least bit loose and relaxed. I was dirty and cold.

Why didn't they shoot? I wondered. Why didn't they shoot at us? I just couldn't understand why they weren't shooting at us. And then the old man and I crawled out onto the marshy patch of ground between the plowed field and the fence. And then I understood why the Russians in the tower had not fired. They would wait and see if we got by the mines. Sure, there had to be mines there. I held the man a little behind me so I could crawl a foot or two in front of him and try to see if I could find the mines. I wished I had paid better attention to the lecture about mines in basic training. Who listened to all the crappy lectures anyway? We'd been too sleepy and horny to concentrate on stupid things like mines.

And why the hell didn't anyone help us? Why didn't they put down those goddam binoculars and help us? This wasn't some shit-eating spectator sport, this was war. They didn't even come down along the fence. What was the matter with those people?

I inched forward, trying to feel the ground in front of me, trying to figure out the freezing, marshy earth. I looked back at the man, but he wasn't smiling any more. "OK?" I asked.

He seemed to nod his head, although I'm sure he never even heard me. I looked up at the fence again. That cruddy fence. That cotton-picking, shit-eating fence. It couldn't have been more than twenty yards away. Just two quick first downs away. And then the noise came, that terrible noise! I was conscious of being picked up and then slammed down onto the earth—of a truckload of dirt being poured over me. Everything was suddenly bright, and then it turned dark. But, oh God, the noise—the noise—the noise! Oh, God damn! That spinning noise-noise-noise! The noise kept spinning round and round and round.

And then it stopped.

I looked up and saw the sun. I was conscious of lying on my back and seeing the sun. There were dark brown figures all above me. I couldn't figure out what had happened. I couldn't figure out anything. And then I remembered. Yes, then I could remember.

I was at the Brown training camp. We were in scrimmage. Here they come. Here they come. OK, watch for the trap, watch for the trap. The brown-shirted quarterback leaned over the center. "Orange twenty-five," he called out. "O-range, two-five." I braced myself behind the left tackle.

"Set!" the quarterback called. "Hutone—huttwo—hut-three . . ."

I automatically moved to my left. There was a shoulder in my stomach. I twisted and dived toward the opening. There was a tangle of brown and white legs and orange, shining helmets. I felt the sullen thud, the obtuse crack of leather, the scrambled fall. And then we were picking ourselves up off the green turf.

"Who had that middle linebacker?" the squeaky-voiced coach rasped. "Who had sixty-three?"

I readjusted my helmet, then walked back to the defensive huddle. "Way to hit," someone mumbled.

The big defensive coach leaned down into our huddle, his hand on my back. "You OK?"

"I'm OK," I mumbled.

"Right, that's the ticket. I want to hear that leather popping on every play, dammit." I looked down at the ground. "Right," he said again. "Give 'em the middle blitz." He clapped his hands together and the huddle broke. We took our positions, then watched the offense come out of their huddle. They'd call the same play again. They'd come right back at us and try to pop some leather. We shouldn't be blitzing, I thought. We should be playing it loose. That squeaky bastard always called the same play again when it didn't work the first time. But I shouldn't be blitzing . . . I shouldn't be blitzing! They were gonna trap me. I knew they were gonna trap me. And how those guys loved to hit! Oh brother, how they loved to hit. This wasn't college anymore, either; this was absolute war and I shouldn't have been blitzing. It would be slant sixty-four all over again. OK, Jimmy, you just try going through that four hole again, you just try.

I turned and looked back at Andy. He gave me the thumbs-up sign. Jesus, he was scared shitless. "Here it comes again," I said. He nodded and kicked at the turf. How the hell did he get through the first cut? And what the hell was I doing on defense? I wasn't signed to play defense. I was signed as an offensive left guard, I was no linebacker. Ah, pro football was giving me a pain in the rear end anyway. All that hitting by day and bullshit by night. We had more stupid training rules in the pros than at Ohio State.

OK, there they were. Come on, 78, you just try me again,

OK? Oh hell, I was blitzing, he wouldn't even come close to me. They shouldn't have had me blitzing.

"Orange fifty-three," the quarterback yelled, getting over the center. "O-range, five-three."

I started to cheat in toward the center. "Hutone—hutwo . . ." I was off with the snap. The center missed me with his elbow and I reached out for the quarterback. But I was too late. I knew I was going to be too late. They shouldn't have had me blitzing. I *knew* I was going to be too late. The ball was handed off to Jimmy and I knew he was going to cut through the four hole. Yeah, the same damn play. I *knew* it was going to be the same damn play. The hell with it—I knew I couldn't get to him.

And then it hit me! Man, did it hit me! I turned to get away, then heard it snap right then and there. I didn't feel a thing, just heard it snap. Just like that. I fell down to the ground watching the sky get dark, then light again. I was conscious of someone falling over me. I was conscious of thinking that my leg was awfully hot. I tried to get up, but I couldn't move. I tried again, but there was something holding me down. And then I heard a voice calling for a stretcher. Who needed a stretcher? "I'm OK," I shouted. "Just get the fuck off my leg!" And then the Doc was over me, looking into my eyes. "I'm OK!" I shouted.

"Be still, son," he answered. And then he looked down at my feet. All of a sudden it came. Like a big, burning, two-thousand-pound axe. God, it was hot. God, it hurt!

"Christ!" I yelled, trying to get away from the pain. "Oh, Christ!"

And then I saw those dark brown figures looking down at me. What the hell was the matter? "Tough luck, kid," someone growled. "Tough luck, man."

I was OK, what was the matter with them?

"Be very still, son," the Doc said, putting a blanket over me. I didn't want a blanket. It was too goddam hot as it was. I felt myself being lifted up and carried along on a stretcher. And then I knew. I had quit just a little bit too soon. I had given up.

I had also broken my leg.

The cloud cleared up, but there wasn't any sun. I was conscious of the damp, cold, lumpy ground. "I'm OK," I said, spitting out a mouthful of dirt. "I'm OK." I felt down to my legs. I *was* OK. "OK," I said. "We'll get them this time." And then I heard the noise from the stands. Yeah, they were giving old Murray the cheer. Yeah.

And then I remembered. Good Christ, what had happened? A mine must have gone off behind us. They must have shot it off. But where was the shouting coming from? I looked all around. And then I saw the old man. Part of him had been thrown up against the fence. The other part was covered with dirt. I was sick. I was sick all over myself.

The shouting grew louder. I looked off to my left. About ten men were on the other side of the fence, waving and shouting at me. I stumbled over toward them, then fell against the fence. I was sick again, although there wasn't much left to come out.

"*Hier!*" they shouted. "*Hier!*"

"*Macht schnell!*"

"*Schnell!*"

I grabbed ahold of the wire and looked through at the men on the other side. I couldn't remember who they were. But I remembered how to climb fences. I always knew how to climb fences. I climbed up and straddled the barbed wire at the top. And then I heard a sharp crack. And then another. I looked back up at the tower. Those rotten bastards. Those mother-jumping, rotten bastards!

"*Schnell!*"

I saw the dirt fly up in the ground beneath the fence. And then I slipped off. My pants caught on the barbed wire and I cut my leg on the way down. I landed on my right shoulder and rolled over, clutching my leg as soon as I was able. The blood, the dirt, and the vomit all seemed to be mixed together somehow. Some men came over and helped me back up onto the road. That girl was still there, looking at me. She didn't spit at me this time; but she didn't smile at me either.

Everyone just stared at me.

A regular Johnny Wayne, right?

Yes, sir, a regular Johnny Wayne.

Someone helped me back to where the cars were parked. It was just like being carried off the field in the middle of the game. Sort of.

Another person gave me a blanket and then someone else gave me a cup of slivowitz. I don't really know if it was slivowitz or not, but it sure wasn't Italian Swiss Colony wine. I remember having to pee something fierce, but before I could find a place to do it, or a wall, or anything, it just balled right up and flowed on out. It was a helpless feeling, let me tell you. I'd always laughed about people peeing their pants, and there I was doing it.

A little later they put a lot of us on a bus and we rode down into Vienna, then got lost, and finally ended up outside of the city someplace at a refugee camp. They let me keep the blanket they had given me—but later, the next morning, when they found out I was an American GI, they made me give it back. Not that I blamed them any, for when I found out how the old US of A was operating, it didn't make me feel so good. I wasn't a real refugee, anyway.

I'll never forget that refugee camp. Ever. People all over the place asking questions. People crying. People confused. People bringing trains in from France and Switzerland and taking everyone who could fit on board. People from the US insisting that before they would even consider taking anyone, they had to first know the person's religion, marital status, and political inclinations. Also his vocational preferences. Jesus, I tell you when I found out what we were doing I almost went out of my mind. Imagine asking about a person's politics at a time like that! What did they expect—that the Hungarians were going to be Republicans or something? I got into a couple of huge arguments with some of our Red Cross and church people, but it didn't do a whole lot of good. They were sympathetic, but not sympathetic enough to alter any of the red tape.

The day after I came back from my leave, I tried to tell Selly what had happened—at the border and everything—but he just didn't seem to understand. All he wanted to talk about was the election. The outcome seemed to be a surprise to him somehow. It wasn't any surprise to me, I don't see why it should have been such a surprise to him that the Big General won.

Lou seemed to understand about Hungary, but didn't understand the fact that I wouldn't babysit for him anymore. But I was through with that crap and consequently spent the rest of my duty drinking Beck's Bier in the club with everyone else. When you play the Army game you don't really have to think about anything.

When I got back home, being separated from the service down at Fort Dix, nothing seemed to have changed much at all. Mom and Dad were a little older, but that cotton-picking town was still the same. I loafed around for a while, then saw a story one day in the *Times* about some Hungarian refugees who were being processed at Camp Kilmer. The next day I borrowed my old man's car and drove down there to see what was what. It was a mistake. I guess I expected things to be organized over here, but they were more confusing at Kilmer than they had been at that refugee camp in Vienna. It looked to me as if those people were being processed into the US Army or something, rather than helped out. One thing was certain, though, those refugees weren't going to believe any more Voice of America broadcasts—that was for damn sure.

That very next Sunday I went to church with my mother. She really seemed pleased, even if I did refuse to shave.

I paid particular attention to what was being said during the service, too. I listened to every word.

The minister talked about the benefits of positive thinking, especially in regard to its application in the sporting world.

Go on, I urged. Go on.

He talked about the last World Series—how Don Larsen had pitched his perfect game. Jesus, he was saying that the lousy Yankees won because they were thinking positively! What did he think, the Dodgers were all thinking negatively?

He really pissed me off. Really!

Without even considering the alternatives, I suddenly stood up—my hand raised into the air. It was something I had always wanted to do.

I was all set to ask a few good questions, but the minister didn't see me. No one else saw me, either. Oh, I'm sure there were some members of that congregation who knew that I was doing something unusual. But they didn't really see me, you know what I mean?

Only my mother knew what I was doing. And she quietly tugged at my sleeve, urging me to sit down.

So, I said to myself, if that's the way it's going to be, that's the way it's going to be.

"Why?" I shouted out. "WHY?"

I didn't get an answer.

Three weeks later, I was back playing football.

PART THREE

The Big Game

(1963)

1

The car wouldn't start. Here I'd made my big dramatic decision to give up playing grab-ass, yet when I got outside to the car, the goddam battery was dead. I bet that never happened to Johnny Wayne. Big heroes don't go leaving their parking lights on, though—only people like me.

Well, what could you expect? I was getting old—thirty, even. Besides, too much was happening. How could I keep my mind on things like parking lights when so much was happening in the world?

I guess that's one reason why I wanted to get away. Only the lousy car wouldn't start!

The first thing I remember after waking up was trying to see if the sun was out or not. I don't know why it was so important to me, I just know it was. I wanted the day to be dark and gloomy.

The sun was out, though, booming down into that air shaft like anything. It had no right to be out, but there it was. We had no right to be playing football, either, but there we were. . . . Hell, the other league had postponed its games; even State had put back the game with Michigan for a week.

Well, the game was going to be played, we had been all through that. That's why we had had that fight. That's why *I* had had that fight. The only real fight I'd ever been in, too.

Oh, Jesus, I wanted to go back to sleep, but I knew I'd never be able to. I looked over at Chancy, but he was still snoring away. Hell, nothing ever bothered him. I slipped out of bed as quietly as I could and went into the can. I sat there a long while thinking about what had happened, about how ironic everything was.

Chancy heard the toilet flush and looked up at me. "What time is it?" he mumbled.

I told him that it wasn't time yet. He turned over and went back to sleep. God, I wished I could have turned over and gone back to sleep. But I knew I couldn't. So I got dressed and went down into the lobby. It was too early for the team breakfast so I picked up my car and started to drive out to the stadium. I must have turned my parking lights on in the fog by the river—I don't know when else I turned them on. I stopped off at a diner and bought a copy of the morning paper, but that was a mistake. The morning paper was still only concerned with one main subject and I wasn't about to read any more about that. I'd already spent a day and a half on that subject, and that was enough.

When I got to the stadium I discovered that I wasn't going to be the first one there like I thought. I could tell by the cars that a lot of the guys must have felt the same way I felt. And had had trouble sleeping.

Everyone looked pissed off at me when I came into the locker room and I knew how they felt. I hated it when people busted right in on my privacy, too. I knew they weren't pissed off on account of the fight. Hell, everyone wanted to forget about the fight, just like the fight had been some sort of an attempt to forget about what had happened.

I sat in front of my locker for a while, just staring at nothing in particular. Here I was, all ready to start my first game as a pro after six years of professional grab-ass. Oh sure, I'd been in on the kickoff units, but those didn't count. This was the first time I was actually starting a game. And just because of the fight, too.

It was the wrong time to be starting, the wrong time to be playing football. But playing the game was our business; besides, we didn't know what else to do.

•

We'd been out on the field, running through some plays in our game plan, when Tape came running out with the news. At first, we didn't believe it, but later we just didn't want to believe it. There was a lot of talk about calling off the game, but the next day the commissioner said that the former President would have wanted the games to go on, so the games would go on as scheduled. When we got the word we decided not to practice, mainly because we were still so shook up about what had happened. Probably, if we would have practiced I might not have gotten into the fight with Browne. But we didn't practice, and I did have the fight.

I tried to push the car to where I might be able to get a rolling start, but I wasn't able to get it backed out far enough. Finally, Moe the Cop saw me and came over and helped me push. It bucked the first time I tried to start it in gear, but didn't kick over. The second time we got it rolling a little faster and this time when I slowly let up the clutch, the car bucked and then the engine caught, and I raced it so that it wouldn't stall. I slipped it back into neutral, then pulled the hand brake on and let the engine warm up. Moe came over to my side of the car. "Sounds good," he said.

"Thanks for the help."

He looked in at me. "How's the eye?"

"Not too bad," I said. He thought I had gotten the eye in the game, but I had gotten the eye in the fight with Browne.

"Well," he said. "Take it easy."

I said I would, then drove carefully out of the players' parking area. I didn't know where I was going, exactly, back to New Jersey, I guess.

My parents didn't live there anymore, but I still considered it home.

I just didn't know where else to go.

•

All fights are stupid, but the fight with Browne was stupider than most. Browne was one of my few friends on the team, one of the few guys I felt I could talk to. But in a way I was glad it was him I had a fight with, not one of the many guys I couldn't stand.

We'd all been drinking beer over at the Rainbow—even the black players. It was the only time I could remember that the entire team got together for an informal beer. Usually, we'd always wind up going in many different directions, in many different groups. But after the announcement came down from the commissioner's office, we all went over to the Rainbow as a team, abstainers and booze hounds alike. We had the place practically to ourselves so we pulled some tables together and all sat around talking about what had happened.

I don't know how the fight started exactly. One minute we'd been talking quietly together; the next thing I remember is that somehow we were on our feet shouting at each other. For the life of me, I can't remember what really caused it. I guess we were both so frustrated that we just had to take our frustrations out somehow.

It might have been avoided if Ace hadn't tried to break it up. That's what really started us off, that's what caused the first blow, I'm sure. For in trying to push Ace out of the way, I hit Browne—and then he hit me back. He caught me again on the side of the head and I smashed my fist into his nose, but that's all the blows we actually landed, even though we wound up rolling around on the floor.

The guys broke it up before we did any real damage to each other. Browne had a bloody nose, and I had bruised one set of knuckles (and was later to develop a black eye) but the real casualty was Ace: somehow in the melee he managed to break his wrist.

After the fight, we all went back to drinking beer, all except Ace, that is. He went back to the stadium.

That evening we all moved into the hotel for our regular pregame evening routine. After the team meeting the coach told me that I'd be starting. He didn't have much choice in the matter—I was the only center behind Ace. Irony all over the goddam place.

Once we actually got out onto the field it was a little easier. At least we didn't have to think out on the field. We went through our usual calisthenics a little more vigorously than usual, and not only because the weather was cold. We kept in motion, just to be doing something. It was the most spirited pregame drill we had all season.

Some of the guys thought that none of the fans would show up for the game, that there'd be some sort of boycott, but I guess they were wrong. I looked up at the stands and could see that they were filling up as usual. I guess the fans were tired of looking at the TV, and hearing the news on the radio, and reading about it in the papers. Hell, everyone wanted to forget. And what better place was there to do it than the playing fields of Pittsburgh?

The Bears warmed up as determinedly as we did. It wasn't the cold that made us all move so quickly—it was the fear of doing nothing.

When we got back into the locker room, we still kept trying to move around, to be doing something—adjusting jerseys and shoulder pads, taping arms and retaping ankles. Anything, just as long as it was something.

I found myself taking a leak next to Browne. He looked over at me and nodded. I nodded back. We didn't have to say anything. We each knew how the other felt. Of course, we didn't have to have a fight, either, but we had.

Then there was a shout from the trainer's room. Then a lot of people were shouting. We went into the locker room and joined the crowd by the door to the trainer's room. Lou

Jobko, our defensive captain, was shouting something. "Jesus," it sounded like. "Oh, Jesus!"

"What happened?"

He shook his head, then walked over to his stool and sat down. I saw Chancy and asked him what had happened.

"They shot him," he said quietly. "Right on the TV, they shot him."

"Who?"

"That guy, Oswald. Jesus, they shot him right on the TV."

One of the assistant coaches switched off the TV and yelled at the trainers to keep it off. We all stopped moving around, doing things. We just sat down and waited for the game to begin.

"What time is it?" someone asked.

"Almost time," the answer came.

Finally . . . Oh, finally! . . . the coach stood up on a stool and shouted for us to quiet down. We were already quiet, but he didn't seem to notice. "OK," he said. "We're all in this thing together. The best way to get it over with is to go out there and get involved. Bang some heads together. Hit someone."

"Bullshit," someone mumbled.

"We got a shot at catching the Giants, you all know that," the coach stated. "This is a time for thinking about football. You're professionals, damn it, you have to dedicate yourself to thinking about football, nothing else. Now, let's go out there and do a job." He stopped and looked around at us. None of us were looking back at him. We knew what we had to do, he didn't have to remind us. He didn't know what else to say so he started to recite the Lord's Prayer. A few of the guys kneeled and some stools and benches scraped across the concrete floor. Only a couple of people mumbled along with the coach, though. When the prayer was over, we all stood up and put on our hats. It was time.

"One more thing," the coach shouted out. "We go out as a team."

"Why?"

"No TV introductions."

"How come?"

"No TV."

Jesus, they just wouldn't let us forget!

I made a wrong turn and as I was backing around to get in the right direction, the car stalled. I thought for a few seconds that I'd have to get another push, but the battery just managed to turn the engine over. Get it recharged right away, I said to myself. But I didn't stop to get it recharged. I kept right on going toward the turnpike entrance.

There was a GI hitchhiking at the entrance to the toll booth area. I looked at him and started to slow down, uncertain. Then I saw his companion on the other side of him. Small and sort of frightened. And female. I stopped the car, being careful to keep the motor from stalling.

"How far are you going?" he asked me when I rolled down the window.

"All the way," I said. "New York."

He opened the door and let his girl slide into the back seat. She looked at me, but didn't smile. The GI climbed in next to me, putting his duffel bag on the seat between us.

"Want to put it in the trunk?" I asked. He shook his head. "Sorry the car's so dirty . . ." I shrugged and didn't go on. I accepted the ticket from the toll booth attendant, then swung around and onto the turnpike. "How far are you headed?"

"New Jersey."

I looked back at the girl. She was looking out the window. She didn't look too happy.

"Fort Dix?" I asked.

"Yep," he said. "You know it?"

"I know it. What unit are you in?"

"Transient company," he said after a brief pause.

"That right?" I started to ask him where he was headed, but was interrupted by the girl.

"Tell him the truth."

The guy shrugged, looked over at me quickly, then out his side window. I waited for him to say something else, but he didn't. We drove on in silence for a while. The old car whipped down the turnpike smoothly. It was a '55 Ford I had bought from my old man after I came back from Europe. Somehow I had nursed it along for six years, rather than trading it in for a new car. I just didn't like the idea of owning a new car.

"I'm afraid the heater doesn't work too well," I said.

"That's all right," he mumbled.

I looked back at the girl, but she was still staring out the window. Two real winners, I thought to myself. Of course, I wasn't such a real winner myself, not with one black eye, a two-day growth of beard, and a grubby old heap of a car.

I reached the heap's maximum speed of fifty-three miles per hour. I felt him looking at me. "You want me to drive?" he asked.

I shook my head. No one could drive the heap except me.

His girl leaned forward. "He's going back to the stockade," she said suddenly, harshly. "He's going to prison."

"Shut up, Dora!"

I didn't say anything.

When we took the field, the stands were as full as they ever got in Pittsburgh, maybe even a little fuller. It didn't seem to make any sense at all, but I was beyond worrying about what the fans might, or might not, do. We ran up and down the sidelines to get loose. Chancy and I banged our shoulder pads against each other. He kept sneaking looks at the stands. "What's up?" I asked.

He shook his head. "I don't know," he replied. "Some nut could be up there taking a potshot at us."

I looked back at the stands, too. Who knew where all the nuts would be? You go around thinking there's a nut behind every tree, you keep hearing footsteps all the time, why you'd just drive yourself crazy. You had to live your life and take your chances. Sure you did.

A whistle blew out on the field. Maybe we could get the lousy game started. Then we could get the whole thing over with.

The Steelers were receiving so I jogged out onto the field with the rest of the special unit. We huddled on the thirty-five-yard line and Junior Washington said that we'd have a return left. Big deal. We clapped our hands together, then took our positions. I was ready to hit someone, to get it all started, for I knew that was the only way to survive in the pro game. Hit them before they hit you.

We waited for the starting whistle to blow, but then there was an announcement over the PA. We were going to observe a minute of silence. Oh, Jesus, let's get it the fuck started! I took off my helmet and looked across at the Bears. They stood there in a line, looking back at us. The silence was broken by a scratchy recording of the national anthem. Where was the band? That's right, the band wasn't there. No TV. No band. No noise from the stands. It was weird.

I think all of us felt that once we popped someone everything would be all right. Once the game got under way everything would return to normal. When the anthem was over, there was some scattered applause from the stands, but not the usual burst of excitement.

We put our hats back on, snapped our chin straps, and made ready to receive the kickoff. The Bear kicker set the ball up on the tee, then trotted back to where the rest of his team-mates were waiting for him. OK, OK, I said out loud. Here we go. Here we go. Let's get it started.

The whistle blew. Then something happened. The Bear kicker started forward and I braced myself to see where the ball was headed. . . . But his foot never met the ball. . . . I looked up and saw him leaning over the tee. . . . Oh, Jesus, the wind had knocked the ball off the tee. . . . Oh, Jesus, we just couldn't get that game started!

The ball was replaced. The kicker ran back, then raised his hand. He wanted to get it started, too. The referee's whistle blew again, and this time his foot pounded into the ball. I watched it fly over me, back to Junior Washington. OK, here we go. Here we go. I moved back until I was sure Junior had the ball, then picked out my man coming down the field. He feinted to the left, but I caught him when he reversed back to the right. We both fell into a heap, then tried to get to our feet again. I hit him again before he could move out. Junior made it back to the 28-yard line. Big deal. At least the game was under way.

I looked over at the Bear player I had taken out. (Or had he taken me out?) It was Lou Morrison. I had played against him in college. He was getting too old to be on the special units.

"The old man must be scraping the barrel," I said.

"Screw you," he muttered.

Then a funny thing happened. There was a huge cheer from the stands. Lou and I looked around, but all we could see was Junior Washington and his tacklers getting up from the pile. "What are they yelling about?" Lou asked me.

"Maybe they shot someone else," I said.

He shook his head. The fans kept on making noise. "I guess," he said, "they're happy the game's started. Now they got something to do."

He then trotted over to the Bear bench. I started to jog to the sidelines, then I saw one of the assistant coaches waving at me, yelling something. Then I remembered: I was the starting center. I ran back to the huddle and joined the offense. "Call the fuckin' play!" someone muttered to the quarterback.

The game had begun in earnest.

"What did you say?" I looked over at him to see if he was asleep or had really said something.

He changed his position in the seat. "Can we take a break?" he asked.

"Sure," I replied, looking out at the turnpike. "There should be a Howard Johnson's coming up ahead."

"Two miles," the girl said from the back seat.

We didn't say anything else until I pulled off into the parking lot. The GI got out, but I said I had to keep the motor running because of the battery. His girl said she wanted to stay in the car, too. He gave her a mean look, but said he'd bring coffee for all of us.

After he left, I backed out and drove over to the service area.

"Where are you going?" the girl asked.

"Gas."

"I don't have any money," she muttered.

"I got money."

The attendant wanted me to switch off the motor, but I didn't want to take a chance, so kept it running. When the tank was full, we drove back and parked.

"Is he really going to the stockade?" I asked.

She didn't answer. I turned to look at her, but she still kept looking out the window. I turned back and switched on the radio. All I got was static. One of these days I had to fix that, too. She said something else to me.

"He's been AWOL," she said softly. "They're going to put him in the stockade."

"How long has he been away?"

"Almost a month."

"He may not get the stockade," I said.

She looked right at me for the first time. "Do you think so?"

"It's a possibility." I thought for a moment. "Did he miss a troop movement or something?" She nodded. "Where was he going?"

She looked like she was about to cry. She shook her head, then stared out the window. "Korea," she whispered.

Korea, I said to myself.

The guy came back. He had coffee and franks for all of us. We sat there eating for a while. He finished before the girl or I did.

"You want me to drive?" he asked. "Just while you're eating."

I didn't want him to drive—I didn't want to be just a rider, especially in my own car—but I told him to go ahead. I slid over while he ran around outside the car and slipped into the driver's seat. I warned him about the heap's idiosyncrasies, but he didn't seem to care.

Actually, he drove the car better than I did, but I wasn't about to admit it to anyone. "I hate driving through these tunnels," I said, explaining why I was willing to let him drive. "A friend of mine at college got killed in one once."

"They're real bitches," he said. He soon had the old heap going almost sixty. I was going to tell him that the car started to shimmy over fifty-three, but decided not to. I decided to let him drive until the next Howard Johnson's, and that was all.

"Are you married?" I asked.

"Sure am," the guy said. "Three weeks."

"Congratulations."

He nodded. I looked back at the girl. She was sipping her coffee and looking out the window again. Still. "I can take you right to Dix," I offered.

He nodded again. "Great," he said.

"Oh, for God's sakes, Donald," the girl muttered suddenly.

"Knock it off," he replied quickly.

I heard her sigh with disgust and lean back against the rear seat. Finally, I felt him looking over at me.

"She doesn't want me going back," he stated.

"You're going to get put into the stockade, that's why," she muttered.

"I may not be."

"You will," she replied. "You missed a troop movement."

"Shit, Dora!" he exclaimed. I waited for him to say something else, but he didn't.

"It's his male ego or something. I don't know what it is."

"Shut up, Dora!"

"No, I won't shut up!"

He swung out onto the speed lane and passed two semi-trailers. He handled the heap real well, but I could tell he was angry.

"I have to go back," he said to me. "They'd catch up with me sooner or later."

"No, they wouldn't," Dora answered. "We could go someplace where they'd never find us."

"Shit!" he swore.

"Just finish basic?" I asked.

He turned back to Dora. "You know damn well they'd catch up with me."

"Then why did you go AWOL in the first place?"

"To marry you, that's why!"

"Oh, Don, that's not true."

I looked back at Donald. "I don't want to talk about it," he said. "It's all decided."

We drove for a while, passing a few more trucks. It was early, but it had already turned dark.

"I had just finished advanced infantry," he said to me. "I was on a levy to Korea." He whistled something between his teeth for a moment. "At least, that's where they told me I was going."

"You might not get the stockade," I said. "They can't get you for desertion if you come back."

"Tell her that."

She sighed. "You're going back because Kennedy got shot, that's why. Don't ask me why. Don't ask me what that has to do with your going back. Stupid male ego or something. Stupid!"

"Shut up, Dora!"

"Ego!"

"You ever go AWOL?" he asked me.

"A couple of times," I said, remembering the many, many times I had gone AWOL. "I never got caught, though."

"And never turned yourself in, either, I bet," Dora said.

"It was different in my day," I explained.

I wanted to ask him what the assassination had to do with his going back. I wanted to tell him that it had affected me, too.

I turned to him but changed my mind. He was crying.

"It's all right," I said.

Dora leaned forward. "Donald," she whispered softly. "Oh, Donald."

He pulled over to the shoulder and stopped the car.

My turn to drive.

2

I had a strange pro football career. When I came back to the Browns in '58 no one paid much attention to me, but still I was able to survive the final cuts and make the team. I suppose it was because I had put on a little weight in the service, mostly due to that good German beer. Or maybe it was because I was determined not to get injured again, at least not like I had back in that summer of '55. I stopped trying to think on the football field and just let my natural instincts take over—meaning I played the game with reckless abandon. I made too many mistakes to stay as linebacker, but this old coach the Brownies had talked me into learning how to center, especially the snaps for punts and field goals. I became pretty good at that little task; also, I really popped people on the various suicide squads.

Unfortunately, the Browns lost out to the Giants in both '58 and '59, and in '60 I was picked up by the Cowboys in the expansion draft. I didn't last very long down in Dallas and almost gave up the game right then and there, but I was traded to the Redskins in the exhibition season and really liked playing in Washington, although we never came close to being a winning ball club. I got interested in politics, though, and it was fun being right in the center of things. I also started speaking out about some of the things I thought were wrong with pro football, and the country, and somehow I got the reputation of being a clubhouse lawyer. Hell, I wasn't a troublemaker at all—I just wasn't as quiet about my feelings as I had once been.

It might have been a coincidence, but I was traded to the Steelers, in a five-man deal, the next year. At first, this really bothered me because I really dug what was happening in Washington, but later on, after getting into the swing of things with the Steelers, I found their hard-nosed, easygoing style much to my liking. We didn't discuss politics, but we did manage to have a lot of fun.

I almost got married in '62, but cooler heads prevailed. She was an airline stewardess who wouldn't let me touch her uniform. She couldn't count right, either. We had a lot of fun, but I think we both realized the fun would stop once we became married. At least, that was our attitude, so I guess we did the right thing.

In the off-seasons I lived in Cleveland, at an apartment I had rented when I first rejoined the Browns. I took some courses at Case Tech, helped coach track at a private school, and always managed to get in some sort of trip before training camp started each summer. It wasn't a bad existence, but that's all it was, I'm afraid, just an existence.

My parents moved to Florida in the early '60s, so my hometown of Northwood no longer really existed. At least I had no real reason to return there. My home was in Cleveland, and even though I had no real idea what I'd do once my football days were over, as long as I could still charge down the old field with reckless abandon, still snap the ball with a degree of accuracy and dispatch, and stay free of injuries, I didn't have to worry about my future.

And then the '63 season rolled around, and even though we tied a lot of games, our defense kept us in the thick of the division race. It was exciting to be on a winning team again. Your entire attitude changes when you play for a winner.

The three of us sat together in the front seat. Dora held her husband's hand, and after a while, he stopped weeping. We were through the tunnels now and getting close to Harrisburg. When I had gotten this far in college, I considered myself home, almost. Now I didn't have a home.

He wiped his nose and looked over at me. "I haven't cried in a long time," he said quietly.

I nodded. I had felt like crying myself on Friday night, but I just couldn't do it. Saturday night was too late. Saturday night was when I had had the fight with Browne.

"My brother was killed in Korea," I said. I know it was stupid of me to bring it up, especially right then, but I could see no reason to not say it, either. They both looked straight ahead. "Times are changed," I stated. "At least there's no war on."

"A couple of my buddies have been sent to Southeast Asia," Donald said.

"Sneaky troops?"

He looked at me. "That's right. Advisers."

"Oh, God," Dora sighed. "Can't we talk about something else?"

"She doesn't think we should have troops anyplace," he explained.

"Well, we shouldn't."

I drove on, passing a VW bus.

"What do you think?" she asked.

"What?"

"Do you think we have to have troops all over the world?"

"I don't know," I answered, trying to think of a way that I wouldn't have to answer.

"Oh, come on, you must have an opinion."

"Leave him alone, Dora. He said he lost a brother in Korea, didn't he?"

"It's all right," I stated. "I've changed my mind so many times I don't really know what I think." I looked out at the road. "At first, I thought it was a good idea sending the troops to Korea. Back in my high school everyone hated Truman like anything. I think that's why I was sort of in favor of his decision, even before he got UN sanction. Then, when my brother died . . . I guess I changed my mind."

"Let's talk about something else," Donald said quietly.

"No," Dora stated quickly. "You don't mind, do you? I mean I want to hear what you think."

"I was a GI in Germany during the Hungarian Revolution," I said. "I thought we should have called the troops out then, all right."

"Would it have done any good?"

"Who knows? It might have. All we had to do, it seems to me, was to make some sort of gesture. But we didn't even do that."

"Why didn't we?"

"I don't know," I said.

"I can't even remember the Hungarian Revolution," Donald said. "When was it?"

" 'Fifty-six."

"I was only twelve then."

"It happened right before the election," I said to Dora. "Things were all messed up then. There was a crisis over Suez; I don't know what else."

"Well, I don't know about then," Dora replied. "That was a long time ago. I just don't think we should be sending troops all over the world. How many thousands do we have in Europe? I don't know. Then we have them in Korea, Japan, Southeast Asia—it just doesn't make any sense."

"We have to stop them," Donald said.

"Why?"

Donald thought for a moment. "Or else they'll take over the world."

"We're not going to stop them with troops," she answered. "God, you can circle the earth in a spaceship now. We're not gonna solve any of our problems with *guns*." She looked at Donald, but he didn't answer. Then she turned to me. "What do you think?"

"If some country asks us to help them, then I guess we have to help them," I said.

"That's what I think, too," Donald stated.

"Men!" Dora exclaimed. "None of you understand. You all think you're John Waynes playing War."

I laughed out loud. "It's not funny," she said. I knew it wasn't funny, but I still had to laugh.

"We held them to a tie in Korea," I said.

She looked at me. "We may have stopped the Communists, but we sure didn't stop communism. Besides, we still have troops there. If we want to keep our troops all over the world, we can, but it's not going to help us in the long run. Look what happened to the Roman Empire."

"What happened to the Roman Empire?" Donald asked.

"I don't remember," she answered quickly, breaking into a giggle.

"They lost to the Christians," I said. "Seven to six."

They both laughed. "You've been to college, haven't you?" Dora asked.

"How can you tell?"

She smiled for the first time. "I don't know. Intuition."

"Do you learn anything in college?" Donald asked.

"Not much," I replied, thinking of the math I had learned, and of the many football techniques I had somehow assimilated.

He asked me where I had gone and I told him. "They play good football out there, huh?"

"I guess they do," I said.

He looked across Dora at me. "I think you can learn as much in the Army as you can at college."

"Don't be ridiculous," his wife stated.

"I want to know what he thinks."

I thought. "Maybe you can," I said after a few moments. "But only in a limited way."

"What do you mean?"

"I mean there are times when thinking for yourself does not go over too big in the Army."

"Is that what you do in college?"

"I think so," I said. What did I know about it?

What did I know about anything?

Dora said something to me. I asked her to repeat it. She asked me what I did.

"Work," I said.

She smiled. "What kind of work?"

I passed another truck, then swung back into the right-hand lane.

"Do you mind my asking?"

I shook my head. "I'm a football player," I said. "Or, at least, I was."

"Pro football?" Donald asked.

"That's right."

"Who for?"

"The Steelers."

"Is that right?"

That was right, I told him. Dora didn't say anything for a while. Then she smiled at the windshield. "Johnny Wayne," she whispered to no one in particular.

Neither the Bears nor us could get much of an offense started. We always had trouble on offense, but this Sunday it was particularly bad. I was glad I was still on the special teams, 'cause the offense didn't seem to have the ball much at all. I was lucky I was playing a lot, 'cause on the sidelines it was murder. All you could do on the sidelines was sit there and watch the Bear offense go up against the Steeler defense. No one felt like thinking, and very few of the guys wanted to talk, so all you could do was to get your mind blank and watch the game. Fortunately the defense got us the ball back quickly most of the time. It was definitely not a day for sitting on the bench.

In the second quarter, almost everyone started to wander up and down the sidelines, just for something to do. We could hear the fans behind us shouting for us to sit down so that they could see, but we just didn't feel like sitting down. The temperature seemed to be getting colder as the game progressed, so we stamped our feet on the ground, and huddled in our parkas, and prayed for the defense to get us back the ball as quickly as possible.

Usually during a game, I'd sit with Chancy—when one of the special units wasn't in action—and listen to him announce the game for me, and one or two of the other rinky-dinks. Chancy would have made a pretty good announcer, only they never would have let him broadcast over the air, mainly because he told the truth about a game. Also because he used the language the players used. Rarely do you hear an announcer tell the truth about a game. Rarely do you hear one saying who really made the mistakes, who isn't playing so good, or what's really going on. All you seem to get from most announcers is names, numbers, and hometowns, and most of the time they get them wrong anyway.

Chancy told it like it really was, though.

But this wasn't any usual game, so Chancy didn't announce it to us.

During halftime, we all gathered together by units in the locker room and went about business as usual. That is, the coaches all met with each unit, told us what we were doing wrong and what we should be doing right to whip the Bears in the second half. Then the head coach called us all back together and I had the feeling he wanted to wade right into us, like he sometimes did, but that he just wasn't able to. I could tell he was as angry and as frustrated as any of us were, but that he felt—being the coach—that he should try to control things. I think it would have been better if he just let loose and yelled the shit out of us. But he didn't. And we began the second half with another prayer.

We might have been able to forget; but the prayer made us remember.

The fans cheered when we came back out onto the field. With no halftime entertainment, they were anxious for something to do, for something to participate in. At least we had kept busy in team meetings; they had nothing to do but stare at an empty field.

But as I snapped my chin strap on for the second half kickoff, I knew that it was only a matter of time before I had to do something. Maybe even chuck the whole stupid business.

We stopped for some more coffee, just east of the Harrisburg exits. This time I went to get it while they stayed in the car, making sure that it didn't stall. Donald asked me if I wanted him to drive again, but even if I was a little stiff from driving, I didn't feel like letting him drive. Hell, it was my car, wasn't it? We sat in the car, sipping coffee, and then they went in to use the can and, a little later, we were again on the way. I asked him if he had to be at Dix at any special time. He smiled and shook his head.

"They'll take me whenever they can get me, I suppose," he replied.

Dora sighed.

I tried the radio again, but all I could get was static. Donald said it was probably just a loose wire and asked me if I wanted him to try and fix it. I told him it wouldn't be necessary. A car radio wasn't all that important, but it would have been better than talking about football, 'cause that's what he wanted to talk about.

"You really play for the Steelers?"

I assured him that I did, or had. He asked me what position, and I told him.

"That's really great," he kept saying. Dora didn't say anything else about it. At least for a while.

Then she had to ask the inevitable question: "You didn't play this afternoon, did you?"

I looked over at her for a second, then back at the turnpike. "Yes," I said. "We played this afternoon."

"You're kidding!"

"I'm afraid not."

"You mean they actually went ahead and had the game as usual?"

"That's what he said, Dora."

"I'm asking him."

"No one wanted to play," I stated. "But we didn't have much choice."

"You could have refused."

"Refused what?"

"Refused to play."

I shook my head, deciding not to pass the truck in front of me. I wanted to change the subject because I knew she was right. How come these kids knew what was what and weren't afraid to say so? "We're all under contract."

"So?" She smiled when she said it, though. "That doesn't mean you had to play."

"Leave him alone, Dora," Donald said.

"No, I'd like to know. You don't mind, do you?"

I smiled. "No, I don't mind. You know, none of us—none of the players—thought there'd be a game today. Then when the commissioner passed the word down that everything was going to go on as usual, why we were all pissed off. But you want to know the truth? I think all of us were a little glad, secretly. I mean, we didn't want to play, but we just didn't know what else to do. It was better than just sitting around another day . . ." I stopped and passed the truck, finally. "It was probably wrong, but we just didn't know what else to do."

I didn't tell them about my fight with Browne; that was my affair.

She shook her head. "Don't you have any rights, or anything? Don't you have some kind of organization?"

"Yep," I said. "But the commissioner has the final say in everything."

"Who chooses the commissioner?"

I laughed. "The owners," I admitted.

"God," she sighed.

"What difference does it make if he played or not?" Donald asked her suddenly. "Geez, leave him alone."

"You're the one who was all excited about everything," she retorted. "You're the one who's making this grandstand play about going back to the Army and everything."

"Well, that's exactly what I mean. There are some things you just have to do, that's all."

"Men," she sighed. She tried to stretch out, but couldn't, so she sighed again.

"You want to lay down in back?" I asked.

She put her hand on my knee for a second, by mistake, then jerked it off quickly. "You're nice," she said. "I suppose all the people came to see the game, too?" I nodded.

"Bigger crowd than usual."

"God," she sighed. "Football!"

"What do you want everyone to do?" Donald asked. "Go in mourning for a year? Life has to go on." He slapped the dashboard with a gloved hand. "Some things we just have to do."

"I don't accept that, Donald. All I want is for people to act sensibly. It's not very sensible to be fighting people all over the world. It's also not very sensible to be playing football at a time like this."

"That's stupid," Donald said. "Stupid."

No one said a word for several miles. I had the old heap going almost sixty, too. It was faster than I liked to drive, but at least it kept me occupied. I wanted to explain to her—hell, to both of them—my real role in the game, but I wasn't so sure I could communicate it properly. It might not have helped them reach a reconciliation, either. Married only a couple of weeks and already arguing. When I had been their age what you looked for in a potential mate was sincerity and that good glow of togetherness. You certainly wouldn't consider someone who didn't agree with you on major issues. Maybe that's why I hadn't married. They were awfully young, too. And he was probably going to wind up in the stockade. I had been prison chaser a couple times at Dix when I was in radio school. The stockade wasn't much fun, and no place for a married man, regardless of his age.

But could I tell him not to go back? Hell, I didn't know. Why had he gone AWOL in the first place?

I looked over at them, then back to the front. When I looked again, she met my eyes. "Could I ask you a question? Donald?" I said.

"Sure," he said.

"Why did you go AWOL?"

I could see him shrugging. "To get married."

"That's not true, Donald."

"It is," he replied. "Her parents were away. Out in Ohio working at some factory. If they'd been there I wouldn't have stayed—I would have gone back."

"Oh, Donald, that's not true."

"It is."

She shook her head, then turned to me. "He didn't want to go back, really he didn't. He hates the Army, only he wouldn't admit it to anyone. Why do all men pretend they like things? Why do they always go out of their way never to admit they're wrong?"

"I don't know," I said, smiling—sorrowfully, I think.

"They beat him up in basic training . . ."

"Shut up, Dora."

"No." She turned back to me. "They beat him up and everything and it wasn't even his fault."

"C'mon, Dora."

"He took the blame for someone else, and they beat him up, and that's why he wasn't going back."

"I stayed to marry you."

She shook her head angrily. "That's not true, Donald, and you know it. We were going to get married anyway, whether you went back or not. We were going to go up to Canada and . . . oh, I don't know." She reached up and touched the corner of her eye. "Then there was the assassination and he decided to go back." She turned to her husband. "My parents being away had nothing to do with it."

"Oh, geez," Donald moaned, looking out the side window. "It's all decided."

We drove on. A little later I saw her put her hand over and take his. At first, he pulled his away, then—the second time she tried—he held onto it. They looked at each other, then he slipped his arm around her and she snuggled up against him. They were going to be all right.

I looked over at them again and smiled.

They didn't look back.

"LOOK OUT!" he shouted suddenly.

I slammed on the brakes, but it was too late. The car swerved, but it didn't swerve quickly enough. There was a loud PLOP, and then the car shuddered and swerved over to the right.

Jesus! I had hit something.

I guided the heap onto the shoulder, its engine already stalled, then switched off the ignition and the lights.

"I could tell the right front tire was flat.

"What was it?" I asked.

"I think it was a deer."

Jesus. I opened the door and looked at the front of the car. It was cold out and felt funny to be walking around. The front right fender was severely dented, the headlight smashed, and the tire flattened. "Well," I said, "not too bad."

I heard them talking, back behind the car a ways. "Oh, God," she called out.

"Help us," he shouted to me.

I walked back to where they were. "What is it?"

"It's gonna die," she wept.

"What is?"

"The deer." She grabbed ahold of my arm. "We have to do something."

I looked over at Donald, then back at my damaged right front end.

I wasn't sure I knew what to do.

3

I went back to the trunk and rolled the spare tire out. I was just starting to jack the front up when he came over to me and grabbed my arm. "What are you doing?" he asked, angry at me for something.

"Changing the tire, what do you think?" I leaned down to adjust the lug wrench, but he pulled me away. "What's the matter?"

"That deer is dying," he shouted. "We have to do something."

"We can't do anything."

"We have to do *some*thing!" he pleaded. "We have to!"

I dropped the wrench. "OK," I said. I walked back to the deer. Dora was sitting next to its head, stroking it gently. Suddenly it tried to stand up, but it wasn't able to. It looked like I had run over its two rear legs.

"What can we do?" I asked the deer.

"Oh, I don't know," Dora wept. "I just don't know."

"I've got a blanket in the car, I think."

"A blanket won't help."

I didn't know what else to offer. What do you do to help fix a broken deer? I looked back at the cars whipping along the turnpike, roaring by without noticing us. We stood there, looking down at the deer for a few minutes more, trying to decide what to do.

"Oh, God!" Dora called out, then started to run out to the roadway.

"Hey!" Donald said.

She tried to wave down a car, but no one stopped. Heck,

by the time they saw her, they were already past.

"Be careful," Donald warned. We looked down at the deer again. It was still breathing, but it wasn't making any further attempts to get up.

"Here comes something," Dora called back.

We walked up to the turnpike and saw the flashing light of a state trooper. He saw us and pulled over. Dora ran up to him and pointed back to the deer. The cop got out of the car and looked over at us, then at my car.

"Whose car?" he asked.

I walked over to him. I told him it was mine. Dora kept talking about the deer, but he didn't pay any attention to her. He asked me for my license and registration. I gave him my license, then walked over and took the registration out of the glove compartment.

"He's dying!" Dora called. "Hurry."

The state trooper looked at both cards, then handed them back to me.

"What's taking you so long?" Dora shouted.

The trooper looked at my car, at the front right headlight and tire. Then he walked slowly down to where the deer was. He kneeled down next to its head, then looked at its damaged rear legs.

"What can we do?" Dora asked.

"Nothing," he said, standing up.

"Can't we help it?" Donald whined.

The trooper shook his head. "Stand back."

"What are you doing?"

"Have to." His hand went to his holster. Dora saw what he was doing and tried to stop him. He pushed her gently away. "Stand back."

Donald held onto his wife while the trooper leaned over the deer.

"You bastard," she cried. "You don't have to shoot him."

He looked at her for just a second. "I can't fix him, lady, no one can."

"But you don't have to kill him, do you?"

"He won't feel a thing."

"How do *you* know?" she asked, crying.

There was only one shot. The deer quivered and scratched at the ground, and then was still. "Good thing it's still deer season," the trooper chuckled. He then walked briskly back to his car and used his radio to make a report. Donald and Dora didn't move. I walked back to the heap and finished changing the tire. The trooper drove up to where I was, and lowered his window on my side. "Get that headlight fixed," he told me.

I didn't say anything. He looked at me, then drove back onto the turnpike. Then I remembered. "Hey!" I shouted after him. "Hey, wait!"

But he was gone. He probably wouldn't have given me a push anyway. I closed the trunk, then tried the ignition. All I got was a clicking sound. Oh, Jesus, now what?

Donald and Dora came over and helped me push the car. The first time it didn't kick over. I forgot to turn on the ignition. Then I told Dora to take the driver's seat and told her what to do. Donald and I got the heap moving, and when she let out the clutch, the engine caught. She moved off about thirty yards, shifted into neutral and raced the engine. I asked her if she wanted to drive for a while. She shook her head. I looked over at Donald, but he didn't want to drive, either.

I got back into the front seat and drove off. We didn't talk anymore. I kept my eyes on the road and stayed under fifty. We weren't in any hurry.

We kicked off to start the second half. I lined up with the rest of the guys, waiting for the ref's whistle. I knew what I had to do—charge right into the Bear wall—but something was different. Something was wrong.

The whistle blew and we took off down the field. I sidestepped one Bear player, then checked to see which side they had the play on. I saw the wall form in front of me and I lowered my head and blasted into it as hard as I could. I heard all the usual grunts and groans, and pads popping on pads, and curses.

But something was different.

I didn't stop the ball carrier; someone else stopped him on the 26-yard line. I picked myself up and looked at the players around me. One of the Bears winked at me, then trotted off the field. I looked around again, unsnapped my chin strap, then started to walk off the field.

When I got back to the bench, I knew what the trouble was. I had had it with professional football. All of a sudden, nothing made any difference to me any longer. I decided right then and there that I wasn't going to hit anyone anymore. I'd try to do my job as best as I could—but I wasn't going to try to hurt someone else. I could do my job without hurting someone, and if I couldn't—then the hell with it.

This wasn't a secret peace I negotiated with the Bears; this was simply a peace I made with myself. There just didn't seem to be any sense in trying to hurt someone playing a kid's game. Maybe I would have done something else if it had been any other Sunday. Maybe I never would have come to terms with the game if I had played for Mr. Lombardi, or been on one of those good Giant teams. But I was on the Steelers, and I'd do my job, but that was all I'd do.

This was no time for any more violence.

The trouble was, though, no one noticed anything different in my play. I snapped the ball well, I blocked, and I did my job on the special units. My secret peace didn't seem to make any difference at all.

Then, later on in the third period, we got the ball deep in our own territory. We were held for three plays and a punt was called for our last down. I lined up over the ball, adjusting it carefully in my hands. I checked to see where my man was, then looked back through my legs at the punter. When the signals were called I looked forward, counted two to myself, then snapped the ball back sharply, quickly.

Right away I could tell that something was wrong. I could tell it by the way the Bears all sort of slid off our blocks and covered to the side. I thought for a second that they were setting up a return, but then I knew that something must have gone wrong with the snap. I looked back and saw our punter scrambling for the ball, pursued by a horde of Bears. When the play was called dead, the Bears had first-and-ten on our nine-yard line.

I slowly walked over to the sidelines. My secret pact had had nothing to do with the poor snap. I was sure it hadn't had anything to do with it. I was waiting for someone to say something to me. I was just waiting for it.

But no one said a word. At least not to me. Not directly. They were disgusted; well, that was all right, I was disgusted myself. I took my helmet off and slowly let it drop down onto the ground.

I was never again to put it on.

"Can we stop?" he asked. It was the first anyone had spoken in quite a while.

"Hungry?"

He shook his head. "Piss call."

We had breakfast anyway, taking turns making sure that the car didn't stall.

Dora looked over at me while Donald was inside. "You don't have to take us all the way to Dix."

"It's all right. I'm going in that general direction anyway."

She shrugged and curled up in the seat. "I don't see why he shot the deer. It didn't make any sense."

"Maybe it was better that way."

"Do you really think that?" I shook my head. "We could have done something," she stated. "We could have tried."

"He probably has to do it all the time."

She turned to me. "Would you have shot the deer?"

"Maybe," I said. Then, a little later: "No. No, I guess I wouldn't have."

"I wouldn't have," she declared. "It just isn't right."

"It's over now."

"I know, I know. But I wonder what that deer felt? I wonder what he would have had to say about it?"

"I should have kept my eyes on the road," I said. "It was my fault."

"It was no one's fault," she whispered.

I didn't tell her, though, that if Donald hadn't shouted out a warning, there wouldn't have been all that fuss. I would have most certainly killed the deer in an instant. The heap would have been wrecked, but at least we wouldn't have had a moral dilemma.

And if the rabbit hadn't stopped to take a shit, he would have caught the turtle.

The Bears scored two plays later. The special unit put their hats back on, but I didn't. One of the assistant coaches came over and slapped me on the rear end. "No sweat," he whispered. "We'll get it back."

I told him to go fuck himself.

He looked at me in disbelief. "Take it out on the Bears," he said, smiling suddenly. "Go out there and knock someone down." He just didn't understand.

The Bears kicked the extra point, then the special units took the field. He whacked me on the butt again. "C'mon,

Big Team," he said. "C'mon!" He clapped his hands together, churning up his enthusiasm. "Let's go!"

I wasn't about to go anywhere.

"Hustle, hustle, hustle," the coach shouted. "Get it back, get it back. All the way!"

I looked at him—all enthusiasm and energy. The crew-cut All American Boy who was an assistant coach only because he couldn't cut the mustard.

"Go fuck yourself," I whispered, then bent down and picked up my helmet.

"Get out there, Murray," someone shouted. "Hustle."

But I didn't hustle out there. I walked behind the bench, toward the tunnel going underneath the stands. Just before I got to the entrance, one of the trainers ran up to me. "You OK?" he asked.

"No," I said.

He looked at my legs, then over the rest of me. "What is it? The knee? The eye?"

"No," I said.

He turned my head from side to side, then broke some smelling salts under my nose. "Get away!" I shouted.

"What's the matter?" He looked worried. The teams were lined up for the kickoff. "What's the matter?"

"Nothing," I replied, going into the tunnel.

"Criminy," he whispered. "At least look like you're hurt."

"Why?"

He didn't say anything. He took my arm and led me through the tunnel and into the locker room. Some of the special police and maintenance men applauded as we went by.

The trainer left me in the locker room, then rushed back out onto the field. I sat in front of my locker, slowly taking off my cleats. Then I looked around; an assistant trainer was listening to the game on the radio, untying a package of towels. Ace Wilson was there, too, his arm in a cast.

"How's it going?" he asked me.
"Good," I said.
The clubhouse man came into the room and whispered something to the assistant trainer. I could feel them looking over at me. "That's right," I said. "I'm quitting."
"You're kidding," Ace stated.
No, I wasn't kidding. I stripped out of my uniform, considered taking a shower, then decided not to.
"Hey," Ace said. "Did you walk right off the field?"
"That's right."
"Well, who's centering then?"
"I don't know," I said. I didn't either. I hadn't even thought about that. I got into my street clothes, then searched through my wallet. I took out a twenty and gave it to the clubhouse man. I told him I'd send some more for the rest of the boys.
I started toward the door. "Hey, Pete," Ace called to me. "You just can't leave like that."
"Yes, I can."
He tried to think of something to say. He didn't have to, though, the assistant coach burst in through the door to the tunnel. "Get your ass out there!" he shouted.
I didn't say anything.
"You leave and you'll never play pro football again," he warned. That was the general idea. He made a move to grab me, but I waved his hand away. He saw I wasn't kidding. Also, I outweighed him by about fifty pounds.
"What about your team-mates," he shouted. "Don't you even care about them?"
"They'll do all right."
"You just can't walk off the field. You have a contract . . ."
I gestured again. "Take your contract and shove it."
He stared at me, then tried a different approach. "Look, Pete," he said. "You quit at this, you'll quit at other things, too. You don't want to go through life a quitter, do you?"

"It doesn't make any difference anymore."

"What kind of example are you setting for the kids, though?"

"Who?"

"The kids."

I shook my head. I was setting them the same kind of example I had been setting all along. What kind of example was pro football setting?

"Oh, go ahead," he shouted disgustedly. "Go ahead and quit, you goddamned Communist!"

I guess that was the worst thing he could think of to call me. I waited for him to think of something else, but he couldn't, so I just left.

And then, when I got to my car, it wouldn't start.

They wanted to pay the tolls for the turnpike and then the bridge over the Delaware, but I knew they didn't have any money so I wouldn't let them. There was a new, four-lane road heading into Dix, but I remembered that route well. Heck, the first time I'd ever gone to Dix (as a GI) was over that same road. We had all persuaded the driver of the chartered bus to stop off at a roadside bar for some beer; when we finally reached the Reception Center we were really flying high. It was the only way to enter the Army. The next morning, after being up most of the night on fire detail, was a different story. I can remember many of my bus-mates crying into their SOS. Beer is one thing; SOS is definitely something else.

I asked Donald one final time if he was sure he wanted to go back. He just nodded. Dora didn't say anything to either of us; she just sat next to her husband, holding onto his arm.

"You should tell them you got married."

"They don't want to hear that kind of stuff."

"It might help," I said.

Donald shook his head. "I'll take what's coming to me, then I'll get the whole thing over with. It was a mistake to enlist in the service in the first place, but I just didn't know any better. I'm not gonna make any more mistakes with my life. We only live once, right? Why does everyone spend all their time doing things they don't want to be doing? It doesn't make any sense."

"You have a point," I replied. "But if everyone really did whatever they wanted to, there'd be chaos."

"They've just brainwashed us into thinking that," Dora said. "It doesn't have to be true."

We turned into the base, past the old Reception Center barracks. We drove in silence past the parade grounds, then turned into where I remembered the overseas replacement depot was.

"You sure?" I asked, as we pulled up in front of the unit he had been supposed to report to several weeks before. "Yep," he answered quickly. "They'd get me sooner or later. Who knows what they'd do? They're afraid of people who do only what they want to do."

I helped him get his gear out, then he smiled and shook my hand. "I have to tell you," I said to him. "I walked off the field today. I quit right in the middle of the game."

"You did?" He wasn't sure what I meant.

I looked over at his wife, then back at him. "I quit because we shouldn't have been playing."

He shook my hand again. He still didn't realize what I had done, so I didn't press the subject. He said goodbye to his wife, then off he went. He told me not to wait, so I didn't.

I drove Dora into Trenton, to the Pennsy train station.

We didn't talk for a while, but when we did talk she knew what I had meant, back at Dix.

"Did you really quit?"

"That's right."

"What will happen to you?"

"Nothing. Get called a quitter. Get blackballed from the league. Lose my pension."

"You don't care?"

"Not anymore," I said. "A few years ago I couldn't even conceive of doing it. Now I wonder why it's taken me so long."

"That's something," she said. "I was wrong about you." I could feel her looking at me. "You should have told us before."

"I didn't know how."

"But what will you do now?"

"I don't know. Think for a while, I guess. Try to figure out what's going on."

"Yeah," she replied. "Who knows what's really going on these days?"

We pulled up to the station. She didn't get out. "You know," she said softly. "I have a secret, too." I looked at her. She started to say something, then changed her mind. She shook her head and looked out the windshield. "Let me ask you a question: If you were pregnant and your husband was going to the stockade, would you tell him that you're pregnant?"

"If I knew," I said as carefully as I could, "I might not even consider going back."

She thought for a moment, frowning. Then she tried to produce a smile. "I wonder if I should have told him then?"

It was too late to offer any advice.

She kissed me quickly on the cheek before getting out of the car. She started to walk away, then turned back to me. I lowered the window so I could hear her.

"One other thing," she said. "You know that Johnny Wayne never served in the Army, don't you?"

"Marines," I replied.

She shook her head. "I heard they refused to give him a

commission so he never went in. You didn't know that, did you?"

I allowed that I didn't know that.

"His real name is Marion Morrison," she added.

Marion Morrison? I allowed as how I didn't know that either.

"It's all right," she said, smiling at me. "Really, it's all right."

I hoped she was right.

I didn't know where else to go so I nursed the heap back to my old hometown, Northwood. It was still dark and I drove around the empty streets for a while, not knowing exactly what to do. I drove past my old house on Effingham, but there was something different about it. I guess it was just me that was different. Finally, I drove back under the Jersey Central tracks and over to the high school field. I parked on the hill behind the locker rooms, just as I always had done back in high school with my old Model A. I walked through the gate, then climbed up into the permanent stands. We had been the only high school in the county to have permanent, concrete stands in the '40s and '50s. Everyone was proud of those stands except those cynics who refused to forget that they were constructed by the WPA.

I sat in the top row, then stared down at the playing field. The sun was just starting to creep up. I was trying to figure out my next move when I heard the noise—a dull, moaning sound.

It took me a while to find out where the moans were coming from. They were coming from the inside of the press box. I pulled back the wooden shutter and tried to see what was going on. Someone was lying on the floor, moaning and crying. And also drinking a lot of whiskey.

"Hey," I shouted.

The noise stopped, but there was no other reaction. I was

going to jump into the press box myself to see if I could help him, but he rolled over and stared up at me before I could.

Jesus. It was my old coach: Crazy Ed.

He mumbled something, but I couldn't tell what it was. "Hey," I called out. "Hey, Coach!"

His eyes opened wide.

"It's me," I shouted. "Pete Murray."

He blinked once, then rolled over, knocking his bottle away.

"Hey, Coach! Are you all right?"

"Go 'way," he mumbled.

"What?"

"Get out of here."

"Come on. Do you need any help, Coach?"

He waved his hand at me, gesturing for me to go away. "Get out of here, you little bastard," he growled. "Get out of here!"

I wanted to help him, but I didn't know how. I reached down and touched Crazy Ed on the shoulder. All he did was to grunt something at me, then move over to the other side of the press box floor. I stared at him for a few moments, then slowly shut the wooden shutter.

If he wanted to be alone—what the hell—I'd let him be alone, that's all.

The heap was still running, so I headed down toward the shore. There was nothing left in Northwood I wanted to see. Nothing at all.

I did a whole lot of thinking on my way down, too. A whole lot. At first, I thought about Crazy Ed and my high school playing days. . . . And then I thought about being over there in Germany in '56. I'd gotten a few letters from Steph, but I had never answered them. The last time she wrote, she sent me a birth announcement of their new kid. She also said that Lou was being sent someplace in Southeast

Asia with a contingent of ASA troops. Well, hang in there, Lou. Hang in there, Steph. . . .

And then I thought about that Hungarian border and, finally, what had happened on Friday. You could think about any number of things, but you couldn't forget what had happened on Friday.

When I arrived in Seaside Heights I parked as close to the boardwalk as I could. I switched the heap off, not caring whether it started again or not. I walked down to the end of the boardwalk, then out onto the beach. There were some kids out there, playing touch football in the sand. I watched them for a while, then asked if I could play. Sure, they said.

At first they complained when I played too rough, when I busted a couple of them a little too hard. "Hey," they called out to me. "It's only a game, man."

I nodded. I knew.

Then, after about two hours of steady football, they complained when I said I was quitting.

"Hey, keep playing, man," one of them shouted to me.

"I'm beat," I said. I was, too.

"Well, we ain't quitting," he said.

Good for them, I thought. If I hadn't been so tired I would have kept right on playing. But I was really bushed, so I quit.

I walked along the beach until I came to some dunes, then climbed to the top of the highest one and sat down. I shivered and watched the November sun shimmer over the shiny Atlantic.

Maybe everything will be better off now, I thought. Maybe we've turned the corner. What the hell, things couldn't get any worse, could they? I don't care what anyone says about the importance of winning—you really only learn something when you lose.

And now we'd lost a whole lot.

Yeah, so maybe now everyone would stop playing games and begin to get organized.

Sure, I said to myself. The game is all right as long as you remember that it's just a game—not a way of life.

I stood up and heard the shouts coming from the direction of the game. "Goodbye, Bobby Thomson," I called out. "Goodbye, John Wayne!"

I charged down the dune, then scampered up another. "Korr——eeeee——aaaaa!" I sang out. "Korr——eeeee——aaaaa!!"

No sir. No one could ever call me a quitter. No way. How could anyone call me a quitter? What the hell, my real life was only beginning.